ONE
LAST
SONG

Biography

Nathan Evans is a writer and performer based in London. Publishers of his poetry include Royal Society of Literature, Fourteen Poems, Broken Sleep, Dead Ink, Impossible Archetype and Manchester Metropolitan University; his debut collection *Threads*—a collaboration with photographer Justin David—was long-listed for the Polari First Book Prize 2017, his second collection *CNUT* is published by Inkandescent. Publishers of his short fiction include Untitled, Queerlings and Muswell Press; *One Last Song* is his debut work of long-form fiction.

Nathan's work in theatre and film has been funded by Arts Council England, toured with the British Council, archived in the British Film Institute, broadcast on Channel 4 and presented at venues including Royal Festival Hall and Royal Vauxhall Tavern. He hosts BOLD Queer Poetry Soirée, and has chaired/hosted events for National Poetry Library, Charleston Small Wonder Festival, Stoke Newington Literary Festival and Rye Arts Festival; he teaches on the BA Creative Writing and English Literature at London Metropolitan University, and is editor at Inkandescent.

www.nathanevans.co.uk

Praise for *One Last Song*

'An enchanting romance—funny, touching and inspiring'
STEPHEN FRY

*'It's very funny, very touching and has the absolute ring of truth about it.
One can't but fall in love with these two more or less impossible people, as
they fall in love with each other.'*
SIMON CALLOW

*'Adored this book and couldn't put it down. An unapologetically queer
love story set in a care home. Touching. Heartwarming. Funny. Sad.
Beautifully drawn characters I wanted to spend more time with. It was
over too quickly for me. Joan and Jim, and their burgeoning relationship
will stay with me for a long time. I loved it.'*
JONATHAN HARVEY

*'One Last Song is a necessary love story, both profoundly moving and
profoundly optimistic. It will almost inevitably infiltrate your heart.'*
MARTIN SHERMAN

*'A warm, joyful and ingenious tale of gay love
from the UK's Armistead Maupin.'*
JOELLE TAYLOR

*'When we forget our gay elders and the radical queer people who lived so
we could fly, we forget ourselves. Nathan Evans has not just remembered
these elder angels, he has painted them with humour, love, truth and
glory. This is a gem of a novella.'*
ADAM ZMITH

*'One Last Song is a beautiful, smouldering, hilarious and sparkling
testament to queer intimacy and the revolutionary potency of queer
creative activism. Every page filled my heart with Pride.'*
DAN GLASS

Inkandescent

First published by Inkandescent, 2024

Text Copyright © 2024 Nathan Evans

Cover Design Copyright © 2024 Justin David

Artwork Copyright © 2024 Nathan Evans

A CIP record for this book is available from the British Library

Printed in the UK by Severn, Gloucester

ISBN 978-1-912620-28-9 (paperback)
ISBN 978-1-912620-29-6 (ebook)
ISBN 978-1-912620-30-2 (audiobook)

1 3 5 7 9 10 8 6 4 2

www.inkandescent.co.uk

for Winifred Baker, in St John's Home
still living in spectrum

ONE
LAST
SONG

Nathan Evans

inkandescent
celebrating diversity

Joan

Well, get her! Hair to shoulder, legs forever, precipitous platforms and a placard proclaiming *Gay Liberation*.

Of course, my hair was hennaed. Can't tell from this picture. Black and white. Grey really, beneath the patina of soot. I give it a wipe, take a better look. And what a looker I was. Not that I could see it then. That jawline, that denim—looks like it's been painted on. Must've been, what… seventy-one? No. Seventy-two. The first London Pride demonstration. When it *was* still a demonstration. When I was still a young man.

The honk of a horn disturbs my contemplation; these old eyes take their time adjusting: my long distance is shocking. Fortunately, this room is not a large one, and I have never been a size-queen.

'He's here!'

Gladys—née Gareth—steps into focus, buttoning a salmon-pink blazer. 'I'm going down.' Not the first time she's used that line, I'm certain. 'Now, put that photograph back where it came from.' Gladys has always liked to take control of a situation. Except in the bedroom. 'And do make sure you've got everything—there's no coming back if you forget something this time, Joan.'

She swooshes her scarf over shoulder, as if exiting some antique drawing room drama; I pull my face up as she pulls the door shut, then put the photo back in the box where I found it. She's right, of course; I am forgetful these days. I've been known to leave the house without my keys, my dignity. And poor Gladys has picked up the pieces. So I shouldn't bitch—she's my last friend left. More cocks up her than she's had hot dinners, but somehow it never got her. It got all the others.

Oh dear. I promised *no tears*. But it's overwhelming, all of a sudden, all alone in this room. A room that's been home half a lifetime—like me, long past its prime. Almost forty years, I have lived alongside this furniture. And the scenes it has seen! The men! The conflagrations.

Well, that was it for the housing association. *Dozy mare— dosing off whilst partaking of marijuana nightcap.* Caught one of the throws and up it went in smoke. I came to, thinking I was in Heaven, dry-ice swirling, and lay, waiting, for 'Disco Inferno' to kick in. But no, my clubbing days are done; it was only the neighbours calling 999 that saved this old gammon.

So now it's been deemed I require around the clock attention. Previously there was a sporadic succession of thin-lipped women trained by Stalin. Making certain I was eating properly. Tying my shoelaces. Authority is never something to which I've responded positively—tell me to do anything, and I shall likely take an equal and opposite course of action. Got me thrown out of home at fifteen. It's getting me thrown out again.

There's the stairs. Footsteps, two pairs. Better pull myself together. As I always have done. When Michael died. And Martin. When I got arrested that time.

My slacks are cerulean, belt and braces tightened. My shirt, cerise chiffon—could use an iron. So too this saggy skin. I put on the best face I can, cap it with my bestest yolk-yellow bonnet. My appearance arrests in-track the disappointingly portly gentleman for whom Gladys holds the door open. I assay a curtsey as I greet him. 'And you must be the porter, I presume?'

If he has a name, he doesn't give one. Probably just as well as

I would only have forgotten it by the time he'd taken one box and returned for the next. There are quite a number of them, piled and packed with what remains of my earthly possessions. They've been somewhat strict about volume and contents. Regulations I took some satisfaction in flouting. The inferno, though, has made editing easier. *My name is Joan, and I am a hoarder*. Comes from a childhood of going without, *my dear*. Imagine—seven of us in one rented accommodation! And this is before London's East End became glittering. Now it's all organic whatnots and shoes with no socks.

Thankfully, my footwear withstood the fiery flames—I favour a sensible flat, these days. Also withstanding, my prize possession—the record collection, sitting ready-to-porter. I can't help thinking they might have sent someone dishier for my big closing number. Donkey-featured and -footed, he trudges in and out, out and in—Gladys flapping around him like she's conducting. Likes to feel useful since she took the retirement, even offers to lift something. He fortuitously declines. At our great age, exertion must be undertaken with precaution. Pull something and you'll be pushing up the daisies in no time.

Though Gladys is but a chicken—been a good decade since I took the retirement. 'All ready, Joan?'

And then there was one. One old bag to be taken down. *No, thank you, I do not need a hand.* I shall take this curtain alone. Though I may take some time.

The building is even more ancient than I am—crumbling cornicing, busted banisters and, of course, no elevator. I swear they've added a stair for every year I've been here, and by the time I reach the bottom, I'm rasping like I climbed a mountain.

I rally and sally into Notting Hill sunshine.

It's not always been home to the starlets and oligarchs; I

13

blame Julia Roberts. When I moved in, W11 was one of the less desirable postcodes in town; then came that dreadful film. I expect the council will sell the flat for a tidy profit. Line their Tory pockets. No wonder they want me out of it.

On the street, Gladys is hand-wringing and a minibus is awaiting. *Well, they might have sent the limousine.* My boxes are all waiting within, and Mister Porter is huffing and puffing with his access ramp down. *I don't think so, darling.* This queen ain't going in the back of no bus yet: I opt for the passenger seat.

It's somewhat further off the ground than I'd imagined. And it is something of a struggle to get the seatbelt fastened. But Gladys, dearest Gladys, comes to my assistance—lets her hand rest on mine a moment too long. I know something is coming. 'Now, John…'

She cannot have called me by that name since about 1971; we were all feminising ourselves back then. Gareth became Gladys, John became Joan; we began experimenting with make-up and clothing. Most men moved on as glam gave way to disco then punk but, for me, it became a mission—my name and my appearance a card thrust into the world's hand, proclaiming revolution. I was not *neither one thing nor the other thing*—I was *everything* at the same time. I was a man who chose to take a woman's name. I was a man who chose to wear both masculine and feminine clothing, finding ludicrous the very notion that cloth cut and stitched in a certain fashion could somehow be 'gendered'. It was *my* clothing, if I was wearing it. It was *my* name, if I was using it. That Gladys has chosen to name-peel— as only she has the privilege to do—can only signal she's about to get real.

'Do *try* to get on.' The eyebrows arch in formation: I have form when it comes to neighbourly vexation. With a purse of the lips, I signal I too have been vexed; Mister Porter-cum-Driver signals impatience by starting his engine. Gladys' head is shaking. 'I'll come see you soon.' She seals my fate with a slam, stands weeping and waving on the pavement.

As the bus pulls off, I do not look back, lest I be turned into a pillar of salt. They might also have put more thought into my exit music. Mozart. Or Wagner, perhaps. Mister Driver is playing some nondescript thump-tchk thump-tchk. And just at this moment, I can't find the strength to ask him to change it.

In these sorts of situations, there's one thing that always makes me feel better. I flip down the overhead mirror. *Oh dear.* That mascara's not as waterproof as the packaging promised. I have a damage-limitation dab at the corner of each eyelid, notice the nail polish is already chipped. *Oh dear, oh dear.* I reach into the handbag on my lap, pull out my *Rouge Allure*. Roll it up like a dog-dick.

Knuckles go white on the gear stick.

I've always enjoyed a *scene*. Making up on the bus. Making a fuss. As I make the pout, lips reddened, I catch the driver's reflection in the rear-view mirror, staring. Let *Operation Shock and Awe* begin.

Jim

He is sitting in his usual chair, its arms worn by others who
have sat there, squinting down at his hand, mottled and veined;
the hands of his watch tell him it is 3.54pm. He has a book
in his other hand. He has been reading the same sentence for
some time: its meaning still escapes him. A *cloud* is in the sky,
surely. A *cookie* is taken with tea.

He reaches for an English Breakfast. His mug—classic,
ceramic—is a reminder of home. Its contents have gone cold.
The contents of his home? He will return to them soon.

Returning tea to coffee-table, he is aware of someone
watching him across the laminated length of the thing. He
adjusts his glasses, eyes adjusting with difficulty to this new
focal distance. *He will get them tested again when he gets home.*
He makes out that woman. *What is her name?* She must be in
her eighties; her dress cannot have been fashionable since that
decade. She is always making eyes at him. In a way he has not
seen since the playground. Or perhaps the office, when they
had first recruited him.

Seeing herself seen, she looks down towards the man in
uniform—blue tunic, brown skin and hair an incongruous
blond. Whatever his name is, Jim cannot recall, and the letters
on his badge are inscrutably small. He is kneeling on linoleum
flooring and painting the woman's toenails. He is painting
them some godawful shade of purple.

The polish assails Jim's nostrils. There is nothing wrong with
his sense of smell. He is reminded of pear drops, always his least
favourite pick 'n' mix. And of the girls in the office; they would

change nail-colour in their lunch-hour as they whispered together.

The woman-in-purple whispers into the man-in-uniform's ear. 'Do you think he is, then?'

Jim's hearing is also still sharp as a pin.

The man-in-uniform looks up at him, smiling. 'What you studying, Jim?' He speaks in that manner they all use with him: like he is a child again.

Jim maintains a dignified silence, returns to his instruction: it is important to keep up with developments if one is to get a position. At this rate, he will never find employment. His eyes slide from the writing like a man down a sheer glass building. Like the ones he built, will build again. If he can ever get his head around this internet thing.

'I know when a man's interested.' The woman-in-purple whispers again. 'Got through 'em like a dose of salts, I did.'

Peering over the parapet of his pages again, Jim sees she is now flirting with the man-in-uniform. She must be three times his age. It is quite obscene. Though Jim *supposes* he can see the attraction. The man keeps himself trim. As Jim has always done. Racket sports are his thing: out on the court on one's own, creating invisible structural models with the movements of one's arm. And then, the winning. By now, his trophies must need dusting. Never too late to add to them, he wonders if South Kensington squash club still meets on Wednesday evenings. He will enquire about re-joining. Just as soon as he is on his feet again.

'That why you got your best frock on?' The man-in-uniform has deftly driven the woman-in-purple's attentions to the arrival of a new man. Arrivals are always a cause of excitement. Especially the arrivals of men. There are currently only two of them on the men's side of the room: Jim and the Nigerian. Or perhaps he is Jamaican. Jim has never dreamt of asking.

'Eighteen down.' The other man is doing something Jim will never do: he is muttering to himself whilst completing a crossword puzzle and, though there is an empty chair between them, Jim can easily hear him. 'Not on either side. Seven.'

Neutral, thinks Jim. But does not deign to say anything. He does not dig foundations; he will not be here long. He keeps his business to himself. And, indeed, his photographs. The other man has spawned snapshots all along the mock-wood mantlepiece—varicoloured grandchildren in varicoloured costumes, who never come to visit him.

The woman in the dressing gown—the one whose needles are constantly clicking—her offspring, on the other hand, never *stop* visiting. On a Sunday morning, she sits terrorised amongst all their ill-mannered children. She is now knitting booties for another of them. Lemon. Yesterday—or was it the day before—the woman-in-purple spent some hours setting down the correct attribution of wool-colour to gender. *Blue for a boy. Pink for a girl. Lemon for everything in between.* Apparently, the gender of this latest arrival is yet to be determined.

The woman-in-purple takes great interest in other people's grandchildren, having none of her own. She constantly bemoans her daughter's lack of a man. And lack of visitations. The woman-in-dressing-gown, poor thing, just sits there *mmm*ing.

That will never happen to Jim. He will never sit in worn pyjamas in a worn armchair. Every morning he gets dressed for the office and combs what remains of his hair. Every morning he scours the job section of the newspaper—as soon as he is out there, out of this retirement he cannot bear, the better. *Proven ability to interpret legislation and implement policy.* Tick. *Proven line management and excellent IT…* Damn it. Back to that damn book. *Getting Online (when you're Getting On).* Or something along those lines…

He is startled by a handclap. He must have dozed off. He must stop doing that. The boss woman is stood in the doorway, hands pressed together before her. She reminds Jim of his first teacher, Mrs Blackburn. Though she never wore one of those headscarf things.

'Everyone. I would like to introduce our new resident.'

The woman-in-purple sits up in her chair, checks her hair. It is thinning, her roots re-growing. She is cooing and fluttering in anticipation of a new man. Another figure steps into focus beside boss-woman. It cannot be described as a man. Or a woman. The figure does not appear to conform to either gender. It is wearing one of those hats—floral, full-brimmed—like Jim's mother used to wear to weddings. It is wearing pearlescent earrings. It is wearing lipstick. Crimson. It is wearing stubble upon its chin. And a ghastly confection of clothing, masculine and feminine. It is called John.

'Joan, please.'

Its voice is sibilant. Its wrist is limp. Boss-woman laughs canned laughter at the correction, like she's in some old sitcom. The woman-in-purple shrinks back in her chair, like she's in a horror. 'This is Eileen.' Boss-woman works in a clockwise direction. 'And that is Mary, knitting.' The woman-in-dressing-gown is openly staring; her needles have ceased clicking. 'Anya, in the corner.' She points to where the woman-who-never-speaks sits, toes knotted like tree roots in the foot spa beneath her. 'Jim, over there.' He uses his book for cover. 'And Harold, here.' The other man—Nigerian or Jamaican—sucks his teeth loudly, deliberately.

'Enchanté.' The creature attempts a curtsy. It thinks it is a clown, obviously. It looks like one, certainly.

The man-in-uniform is alone in finding it funny. 'I'm Craig. The deputy manager.' He offers his hand to the creature. The creature raises the hand to its lips. The man-in-uniform thinks this hilarious.

Boss-woman's look tells him to keep a lid on it. 'Right, then... Joan. Let me show you to your room.' As she leads the creature to the elevator, the only sound is of the spa bubbling between bunions. And as the elevator doors shut behind boss-woman, there is nuclear fission in the sitting room.

The woman-in-purple: 'Is it a man or a woman?'

The Nigerian-Jamaican: 'A moffie man!'

The woman-in-dressing-gown: 'Mmm!?'

Jim stays silent. His eyes stay on the elevator. From where he sits, he cannot make out its digits, but he imagines their journey up to the first floor. He imagines her leading the creature down the carpeted corridor, past the cheap prints of 'cheerful' watercolours. He imagines her opening a door. And he is thinking *that other man only just moved on* and he is thinking *it never takes them long* and he is thinking *please, no, not the room next to mine.*

Joan

Magnolia. Not the flower. Those I adore. End of winter and the branches still bare, it brings hope to this old heart to see their fleshy buds rise proud in the air: life is still there. But the colour. The *colour.* A yellowish-pinkish nothingness—how could anyone think it easy to live with? Not sure I shall manage it. Not for long at least. These walls will be the death of me!

The furnishings I can cover at least. *Granny-goes-funky* is how one might describe them. One of everything—the council have always prided themselves on providing the bare minimum. One armchair. That fabric in which I packaged my trinkets should sort it. One wardrobe, one chest of drawers. How I'll get it all in there I don't know, *my dear.* One single bed. Not been in one of them since I was fifteen and wanking up a storm on mother's linen. One bedside cabinet. Which now has my record player perched atop it. I was particular with the porter about where it should be situated: I knew I should need it right from the outset; if I must unpack, I must have a soundtrack.

I plug in the player and—with only a little light swearing—locate the box containing my record collection. I've just dug out Callas—I do love a dead diva—when there's a knock at the door. *Am I not to be spared?*

For one delicious moment, I deliberate not answering. But then I rally and ready myself for public consumption, *à la Quentin.* How very old-fashioned I recall Ms Crisp seeming, with her blue-rinsed witticisms, while we were out rallying for rainbow revolution. Now my own voice is every bit as querulous as hers once was. 'Oh yes?'

The door opens of its own volition. They've a key to all of them. *A Room of One's Own* this is not. 'Room service!' And in walks that dish—the assistant manageress. Sepia skin straining the seams of an ultramarine uniform. Carl? Colin? Reckon *he's* one of the children—butch, but that blond hair is screaming.

'I don't remember ordering you in.'

His mouth opens. But his eyes are smiling. 'No one round here remembers anything.' Got a sense of humour on him. And a cup in each hand. 'I see you're settling in.' He wends his way between boxes, some open and disgorging colorful contents upon *cream* carpeting.

'It's like home from home.' I put aside the vinyl—more fun playing this one now.

'Well don't go blasting that this time of night. Old dears need their beauty sleep.'

I refocus on the wall behind him. There's some cheap brassy thing, comes with the fittings. Like one *needs* reminding of the clock's ticking. It's eight, no *nine* pm.

'Cocktail.' He offers me a tray: not exactly silver-service—plastic, in fact—the contents of one chalice aqueous, the other candy-coloured. 'Madam or sir, which do you prefer?'

Now, I'm *all over* this non-binary thing the chickens are doing, but I am a man who has taken a woman's name. Which is different. I think. But old stick that I am, I wouldn't want to *say the wrong thing*. So I skirt or perhaps trouser the question. 'I prefer to savour *individual* flavours.' Pluck a pill from his cup. 'What's this one?'

Girl's gotta be careful what she puts in her body. Doesn't want to end up like those drugged-up old dears dribbling into antimacassars downstairs, now does she?

'Enalapril.'

'*Anal*april.' I carefully mispronounce the first syllable—playing innocent, though well I know; they've been on the doctor's order for some while now. 'And what does that do?'

'It's for your heart.'

Dicky—thanks Daddy. 'And this one?' I pluck another pill.

'Reminyl.'

'*Rim*inyl.'

He is *so* laughing. 'That's for your head.'

Offsets the onset of dementia—let's hope I'm dead before I end up like Mother.

'And that one's just a painkiller.'

I am never quite sure which bit of me hurts more. 'Well, bottoms up!' I take the other cup. And they're down in one with water chaser. Done a *lot* of work on my gag reflex.

'Who's that?' He's spotted the picture—Miss Pride nineteen-seventy-whatever, checking it all out from the chest of drawers.

I flutter an eyelash. 'Guess.'

'No!' He looks back and forth in disbelief. The young: never could believe time can touch them.

'I was quite a looker.'

'Not sure about that hair.'

I suck in the stomach and square the shoulders. 'Like 'em butch, do you?'

'Yeah.' His voice drops an octave. 'I like big butch daddy bears.'

My gaydar is rarely wrong. 'So, I'm in with a chance then?' I let my stomach out again.

He laughs. 'I'm a married man.'

That throws me a moment: I'm still not used to it. For me, marriage is all overdressed aunties and overpriced drinks and overcoming one's incredulity as straight boys do the YMCA.

23

Then I get it. He's one of *them*: the assimilationists.

'My husband is horribly jealous of me working around all you hot older men.'

I've only seen two other men since arriving. Neither of whom I would describe as exactly *smoking*. But this one—hotter than a toddy before bedtime. 'And how old are *you*, if you don't mind me asking?'

'How old do you think I am?'

'Sixteen or seventeen?' I err on the legal side of risqué—it's best to, these days.

'I'm twenty-seven.'

'Isn't that a little young to be settling down?' When I was his age, I was taking home anything that wasn't *nailed down*. Not knocking about in a care home.

He shrugs. 'I've found the man I want to spend the rest of my life with.'

'How very heteronormative.'

Well, that shoots straight over his head. 'Sorry?'

'Sounds lovely.' I give him my best pearlescent grin. The message is clear: this audience has come to its conclusion.

He indicates the alarm cord, dangling. 'Call me if you need anything.'

'It's like the Garden of Eden.' I admire his pert bottom receding.

He shakes his head and closes the door behind him, calling, 'Sweet dreams!'

If only. At my great age, sleep seldom comes sweetly. Or swiftly. Now, where was I…

And did I remember to take that Reminyl? Ah, yes—the vinyl.

I decide against Maria in favour of Jessye. Singing the third of Strauss' *Four Last Songs*. As the needle drops, music rises, memories with it. To think we almost didn't get tickets. Peter wanted to give up, but standbys came up at the last minute.

Her voice throws a silken shimmer onto the room. Makes it seem somewhat more like home. *Now that day much tired has made me...* Something like that anyway. She's singing in German, of course. And of course, she's not really singing about sleeping. *...my ardent desires...* Ah, Peter. Held my hand down between the seats—always was 'discrete'. Poor Peter. Then she got buried with AIDA.

There I go again—making a mess of my mascara.

I decide to take Ms Norman's advice, stop everything, and turn myself over to the starry night. Let's see if they're out. I grab the bag—a beaded number I got years back in Portobello Market—pump up the volume and head for the door. I do not mean the door into the corridor—the other door. It is this room's redeeming feature.

These old hands don't work as well as they used to, what with the arthritis and all. The door has one of those new-fangled handles, and I can't work out how to make it turn. Reminds me of when we were touring. Those air-conditioned hotel rooms. I once broke a pane trying to get some air in. I hate feeling trapped. For me, there is nothing worse than that. And I'm panicking and thinking of pulling that alarm when, finally, the door swings open.

It's bijou, this balcony—just enough room to swing a kitty. But it gives the illusion of freedom, looking out as it does over the 'garden'. Just a bit of grass, a few rose bushes. Still, *beggars can't be choosers*, as Mother loved to tell me.

Of course, the garden is the *official* smoking area. What was it Madam said when she showed me around earlier? In that condescending tone of hers—like there's inverted commas around every other word. *Residents who do smoke are permitted to partake out here.* Not in rooms or adjoining external areas. No, not ever.

I reach into the bag—*et voila*—here's one I prepared earlier. A bit bent, but it's done me no harm. *Boom, boom.* Fortunately, no one frisked me at the door for firearms. I light up, and inhale with satisfaction. Simple pleasure number one: rule-breaking.

A therapist suggested I focus on what I am *for*, not what I'm *against*. On what I *do* have, not what I *don't*. So I'm *choosing* to focus on this balmy evening. No stars—it's London—but a sodium sheen. And with Ms Norman in the background, one could almost be at Glyndebourne. Those summer seasons. Those costume fittings. Working my way through *all* those baritones.

Well, that's got me smiling.

Potent as it may be, this weed cannot mask the scent of those roses. Which reminds me... Something else Madam said this afternoon while I was admiring the garden: *Are you always so flamboyant?* I was somewhat taken aback. *Do you have a problem with that?* She seemed surprised by this sudden show of teeth. *Of course not, it is just...* She adjusted her hijab. *I must look out for the wellbeing of ALL our residents.*

And here comes one of them: I hear the sound of a seal being broken and hinges creaking, like I'm in some Hammer horror film. There—on the next balcony over, just about visible through the aperture between frame and door, with matchy-matchy gown pulled over perfectly-vertically-striped nightwear. *Poor thing.* He could barely bring himself to look at me down in the sitting room—book before him like I was some gorgon to be shielded from. Now he's staring.

'Aren't they glorious?' I smile in neighbourly fashion. 'The roses, I mean.'

He keeps staring, open-mouth and everything.

'I'm sorry, I seem to have forgotten your name.'

Like he's seeing the devil before him. I give him one of my best lines.

'I would offer you my hand but alas the distance between us is too vast. Reminds me of the Genet film. What was it called again?' French. Something about love, I think. 'There are these guys in cells and they toss flowers to each other through the bars in the windows. So beautiful.' I saw it down the Southbank a few years back. Released with a new soundtrack. 'And then they blow smoke through a hole in the wall...'

'Smoking—' His voice surprises me, patrician and rather prissy. '—of any description—' He swells up like one of those martinets at London Overground stations who, even though you're stood in the open air, insists you *can't do it here*. '—is not permitted in rooms or residential areas!'

'I know darling, but it helps me sleep.'

'Well, your music is preventing me from sleeping. Kindly turn it down or I shall raise the alarm. Thank you and good evening.'

And like he's in some old made-for-television, the door shudders shut behind him.

Now that's *really* got me smiling.

Jim

Search engine. It sounds like a machine with which one might survey a plot of land. Or send on an expedition for a lost kitten—something with a siren. When he'd heard the wailing that morning, he'd thought it was a fire engine. He'd lain there thinking *something must be burning—I do hope it's not my kitchen.* And then they were there, standing over him in green uniforms. He couldn't understand how they had got in. But as they stretchered him out the door, he saw her: the cleaner. She came on a Wednesday morning. She must have called them.

His mind has wandered off again without him; a knock at the door returns him to the book in hand. *He will get on top of it soon.* He marks his place, clamps it shut, squares scuffed edges to those of the bedside cabinet.

'Come in!'

The man-in-uniform—whose name has again escaped Jim—breezes in with his usual smiles and usual pills. 'Sorry I'm late. Been chatting to your new neighbour. He's quite a character.'

Jim could think of other words to describe that *creature.* 'So I can hear.' All day he has been banging about next door as if to remind Jim of his presence. 'The walls are so very thin here.'

'You should see what he's done to his room—really made himself at home.' The man-in-uniform seems surprisingly taken. 'Unlike some I might mention.' He casts a glance to the suitcase by the door, ever-ready for Jim's departure.

Jim takes his tablets from the man. He doesn't like taking them, doesn't need them, but has always found it best to *keep one's head down.* Then they leave you alone. He cannot even remember what they're meant to be for, as he swallows them, one by one; it takes a considerable volume of water and concentration. 'Joan.' Pausing for breath, Jim says the word as if he would prefer his teeth not to touch it. 'Isn't that what we're meant to call him?' He looks up to find his book no longer on the cabinet, but instead open in the man-in-uniform's hand.

'Who's this?' In his other hand, the man is holding up the bookmark; it is a photograph.

'None of your business.' Jim considers himself a private person. He does not like people going through his things. Which is perhaps why the internet has never appealed to him: he does not like the thought of being *in the public domain*.

The man-in-uniform rolls his eyes, returns mark to book, and book to cabinet again. 'You know, I could always *show* you how to get online.' As if to underline his technical credentials, he takes those things from his ears—what is it they call them—pods or something; Jim had thought them hearing aids when he'd first seen them. Then he'd heard the music, *if that's what one could call it*. Contraptions in pocket, the man tilts his head towards one shoulder to indicate he is about to say something ironic. 'If you ask me nicely, that is.'

Jim does not like asking for things: he was brought up to be self-sufficient. *Why didn't you ask?* they always asked when he couldn't find things in the office.

The fact that this young man has taken out his earphones can only signal there is more to follow. 'Are you okay, Jim?' And there it is: that question. With that look, like they pity him. Is it any wonder he avoids eye contact with everyone? Jim doesn't need to look at the man-in-uniform—now perching on his bed, on its cheap shiny linen—to know he is doing that *thing*, that thing where they pretend to care about him.

'I'm fine.' Hoping that might put an end to it, he focusses on realigning the edges of his book to the cabinet.

'It's just a little bird tells me you've been a bad boy. Not left your room all day.'

Jim has a postgraduate qualification from one of the country's most prestigious institutions; how dare this young man think he have any authority over him. 'I didn't feel like socialising.' The thought of meeting that creature—with all those mincing affectations and unminced exclamations—had kept Jim in his room.

'Oh, that's a shame. Chairobics this morning.'

Jim can just imagine the horror—the mercilessly cheery instructor, that woman making a scene of herself, arms in the air.

'And dinner was jerk chicken.'

Jim has never been one to give much away by facial expression but cannot now stop himself grimacing. He has nothing against world cuisine: he has always enjoyed sampling local delicacies, and some of his fondest gastronomic memories are from business trips to Japan. But the staff in this kitchen should be prosecuted for violating trade descriptions.

The man-in-uniform's voice descends, from the childlike register he has been using into something altogether more commanding. 'Perhaps we should up your dosage again.'

Jim's hands stop fussing; he feels the clean lines of his mind are returning to view again, but whatever they were giving him when he first came in had made a pea soup of everything. Jim appreciates, above all, the sharpness in things: the cut of a suit, the slice of a lemon.

'We'll have to get the doctor in.'

Jim deigns, then, to look at him.

The edge in the man's voice keeps on sharpening. 'You don't want us to get the doctor in?'

Jim has always understood how to play the game, dress the part, say the right thing. He says nothing, but his head is shaking.

'We'll see you for breakfast then.'

Jim's head is nodding.

'Good man.' Sharpness sheathed again, the man-in-uniform gets up, gathers up pill cups. 'You should try talking to Eileen.'

'Eileen...?'

'You know, the one whose nails I was painting yesterday afternoon.'

'Right.'

'I think she's got a soft spot.'

Although Jim has long suspected this, he is quite unprepared for such a comic postscript and feels his face shows it.

'Oh, come on. She's not *that* bad looking. Decent pair. Still got all her own hair.'

The indignity of this description almost makes Jim feel sorry for the woman. 'I don't think it would be right to start a relationship.'

The man-in-uniform does not seem to recognise the closure in Jim's voice. 'And why is that?'

'I... don't think I shall be in this *establishment* long enough to sustain it.'

The man-in-uniform's eyes rotate. 'Right.'

'Goodnight, then.'

'Night.' This time, the hint is taken and, door closed behind him, the man rattles off along the corridor, steering his trolley towards the Jamaican-Nigerian gentleman's room next door.

How could they imagine Jim would be interested in *that*

31

woman? His book must be as closed to them as the one on his nightstand. Jim does not attempt to open it again. In the morning. In the sitting room. It will be a welcome distraction from those lurid soft-furnishings.

Dust must now be blurring the hard lines of his own home furnishings. Unless the cleaner is still going in. *Didn't he set up a direct debit?* He must check. When he gets his online banking up and running. He believes the book covers that in chapter six or seven.

He slips off his watch. Sets it beside the manual. Gold, simple, face somewhat small—it tells him it is early to sleep yet. But he will give it his best shot. He works through the bullet-points of his bedtime routine: one, remove dressing gown, leave hanging; two, remove teeth, leave soaking; three, remove glasses, leave where he can find them. This done, he climbs onto the plasticised mattress and prepares to climb the edifice of sleeplessness.

He must have slipped off, because they're on a beach, possibly Scottish. He becomes aware that their paddling in the shallows is being sound-tracked by something which seems deeply inappropriate. *What is that?* He is sure he recognises it; its accent is more Spanish than Scottish. In trying to identify it, he rises into consciousness.

A woman warbles; an orchestra crashes through the wall. Sleep is now impossible. Jim lies, charging his fury like a battery. How *dare* that creature? Jim would never show such flagrant disrespect towards a neighbour, never leave his rubbish outside another's door. He stares towards the sound a minute— as if the purity of his hatred alone might stop it—then reaches for the light switch, reaches for his stick, and raps the partition between their rooms with its rubber tip—so hard he leaves signatures on already pockmarked paintwork.

He waits for a dip in the music. But the music does not dip. Surely it cannot be *so* loud next door? Surely the creature must have heard? Jim can picture him just sat there, a smile upon those painted lips. He raps even harder this time and can barely believe it when the music matches this escalation, now so loud he cannot but recognise the tune. *Carmen*.

Jim does not enjoy asking for anything, but when he reaches for the alarm cord above him—when he pulls it down, sees it flashing, and knows they're coming—he is smiling for the first time in some time.

Joan

Even at my great age, there is always that moment before stepping on stage when I think *why the fuck do I do this? Why not wear a cardi and slippers like all the other old codgers? Would that not be easier?* And I seek reassurance in the mirror, but only I am there—that blouse, those bangles, that blusher—what was I thinking? And I'm thinking about retreating to the dressing room when the doors ping open—I'm on, and there they all are, watching.

Joan kicks in.

Of course, I am not really walking on stage but into the sitting room; the principle is the same, whether classroom or courtroom or coliseum.

'Ta dah!' As I emerge from the elevator's mirrored interior, I circle the yellow ribbons in my hand. I am not seeking an *ole oak tree* to tie them round, I am...

'Are you John?'

She's there at my shoulder—lapis-dressed, sandy-skinned. Her vowels—Filipino, I would assume—make the John sound *almost* like Joan. And, although I was not expecting to share my stage with anyone, I throw myself into this impromptu improvisation. 'Do you know, you're the first person to use the correct pronunciation.'

I have not met this member of staff before and sense there is fun to be had with her. I offer my hand. Her eyes widen further on noticing the nail polish, but she takes it. I raise her hand to my lips, put on my best Princess Margaret. 'And whom do I have the pleasure of addressing?' Once met the old goer—she

34

came backstage for a tour.

'Eugenia.'

I can see I can run with this. 'And are you a princess?'

Well, the audience are really getting going by this point: that black gentleman (Harry? Barry?) looks like he could kill me point blank as he glowers up from the holy scripture in his lap. *Still got it.*

'Would you like some tea?' Eugenia pulls her hand away.

'Earl Grey, please.'

'I do not know if we…'

'Then I'll just have some builder's.' I tip a wink to the floor.

She hurries to the kitchen with a glance over shoulder. I'm not entirely sure if that's *shock* or *awe*.

'Found some!' I proceed again to the matter in hand, delivering the ribbons into the lap of that woman in the highly inflammable housecoat thing—she is knitting booties in a *sharp* shade of lemon—Mary, that's her name, like Mrs Robinson, like Robinson's Lemon. These days, association is the only way I can remember anything.

'Mmm.'

Mmm is her response to most things. It was certainly her response when, yesterday afternoon, I suggested she might add ribbons, and that I might even have some. Possibly she was simply surprised to be engaged with, poor thing. I sincerely hope, when I am so far gone, that someone will do me the kindness of putting a poker up my rectum.

'Aren't they beautiful?' They are, in fact, from the crown this *Queen of Sheba* was wearing on arrival. But what use do I have for it now?

'Mmm.' Mary is smiling.

But that other woman (Ellen? Helen?) swivels her eyes

35

from the television and in my direction. 'If you're a girl.' She's wearing a sour-milk expression and clothing the colour of a teabag, twice-used.

'Boys like ribbons too,' I inform her. Indeed, I am the authority on this matter. And I go to sit beside the dear old-dear.

But teabag-lady barricades herself across the armchair. 'You can't sit here!'

'Why not?'

'Because!'

'I want to sit next to my friend Mary.'

'Mmm.' Her affirmation, in that moment, means more than a thousand words might have done.

But the tea-lady is having none. 'Sit on the boy's side of the room!'

In a sort-of sexual apartheid not common in this country since the late Victorian era, men sit on one side and women on the other.

'We not want him.' It is the black gentleman, his bible-reading abandoned. 'Do we, Jim?'

I see my new neighbour has graced us with his presence once more. I cannot stand for squealers, *yes sirs*, lady-doth-protest-too-muchers. Look at *her*, with her synchronised socks and neckwear! Got your number, dear.

Jim-Jam looks me up and down, like I'm shit someone trod in, and says nothing.

'I'll take that as a *no*, then.'

He ducks back behind that book he's always reading.

The temperature and my vocal line descend to the linoleum. 'Fuck you!' Inside heat, is rising.

'No, fuck you.' Sotto voce and smouldering, it is again the

black man.

The red mist comes up. The orchestra strikes up. I am Tosca, Brünhilde. I am Elektra. I am advancing on him across the sitting room. Unable to rise to the challenge, he sits, fists clenching and quavering.

The teabag-lady is cheerleading for his team. 'Go on, Harold!' So that's his name.

'Gnnn, Jnnn!' With a departure from her usual repertoire, Mmmary Magdalene joins mine.

That woman who never says anything is wailing quite off-key and out-of-time.

And Jim-Jam just sits there, book mid-air, as I launch into my big aria.

'Darling, I've been bullied by the best of them, from playground to police station, and I simply refuse to be bullied by a dribbling old man.'

Horrid Harold grabs for me. Misses. Never one to fly a flame, I lean in for dramatic effect. Close enough to smell his sulphurous breath. 'And in my experience, the worst bullies are always the closet cases.' Close enough for him to grab the pussy bow about my neck.

My voice drops a further octave. 'Take your hands from the drag.'

He does not.

And I am molten. I am quaking. I am fighting on the frontline. I am coming up, up, up and waiting for the beat to drop.

'What is happening?' The Princess has returned, brew in hand. 'Harold, what are you doing?'

I cannot stand tea from a mug; I cannot stand up.

'I said, take your hands from...'

The beat drops. The heart is a confetti canon. And then

Madam is there and she's saying *call a doctor* and she's guiding me to a chair and it seems to be on the men's side of the room because I seem to be between them, between Harold and Jim and she is asking how I'm feeling, and I'm rallying and delivering my last line to the room.

'There ain't nothing gonna put *this* queen back in the closet again.'

And then, somehow, I am back in my own room.

I have taken to the blackouts with aplomb. Got the practise in when I was young. All that wine and waking in some strange bed with some strange man in the morning.

But now it is night-time. And the Queen of the Night is staccatoing. At modest volume. In Joan *Sutherland*'s heart the *vengeance of hell* is boiling; in mine, it is cooling. No more conflagrations this evening. This evening, I am *chilling*; the only thing burning is one of those candles from the Jo Malone store, gifted by Gladys, Light of Finger. *Lulling Lavender*. It furthermore obscures the scent of geriatric and antiseptic that permeates the air here.

And relax…

On the sleeve on my lap is that extraordinary image of the Queen of the Night descending from heaven on a crescent moon with stars in attendance. I am just skinning up on her, when I hear a rattling in the corridor and a knock at the door. I wonder if I should quickly magic my marijuana away but really, *why should I?*

'Oh yes?'

'Room service!'

The buxom-blond bustles in, humming; I don't look up at him. Once upon a time I could knock out a reefer with one hand but these days rolling requires my full concentration. 'I do hope you've not douched too thoroughly.'

In my peripheral vision, I can see his jaw dropping. 'You filthy…'

Guilty. I've always felt sex should be at least a little dirty.

'Back to your old self, I see.' He tuts. 'Honestly!'

Perhaps he's not the *honest woman* he pretends to be—just at that moment there is the sound of a familiar three-note hook. And *then* I look.

'Thought I'd turned that off.' It must have emerged from those earpieces of his, so loudly even I could hear it. His hand goes to the phone in his pocket and mutes it, swiftly; he smiles shiftily.

I pull a *butter-wouldn't-melt*, but wasn't born yesterday. The apps were not for me: I could never countenance the idea of turning up on some gentleman's doorstep and being turned away. But sometimes, when Gladys came over, she would turn on the Grindr and we'd have a gander.

'What are you doing?' He's now gandering at the reefer in my hand. 'Is that…?'

'Medicinal, yes.'

'Joan…' I can see his mind scrolling the manual for what must be done, but clue there is seemingly none. 'I can't let you do that!'

'Oh, fuck off.'

I see it then, what I have seen in so many men, boyhood trauma written through them as surely as Blackpool or Brighton. The name, the condition, is different from man to man, from generation to generation. I wonder what my words have triggered in this one, teetering on the edge of tantrum.

'Joan.' He's trying to keep a lid on things, but his words are escaping steam. 'I'm just doing my job!'

'Then go get on with it.' I give him *the look of scorn*. My inheritance: how Mother loved throwing them. 'And don't stand there gawping.'

'Joan!'

'There must be plenty of gentlemen to gawp at on your phone.'

And now his jaw is clenching, tendons tensing. Some other person might find this tension unnerving and begin backing down. But not Joan.

'So tell me, are you open, or is it good old-fashioned adultery?' I smile, sweetly. 'And does Boss Lady know you're Grinding on duty?' I lick the papers, slowly. 'I'm sure she'd be tickled pink by your extra-curricular activities.'

This afternoon, we shall call an honourable defeat. But tonight about levels it; I seal the joint shut. This fight, he knows, is lost.

'Just don't smoke in bed, alright.' His voice simmers resentment. 'Don't want *this* place burning down in the night.'

Touché. 'Don't you worry, your secret's safe with me.' I attempt to ease the friction with some friendly KY Jelly. 'And I shall smoke only discreetly.'

I'm not sure I've ever been discreet about anything, but there's always a first time. The gesture has the desired lubricative effect and by the time we're done with my 'nightcap', he seems back to his usual jovial self.

'So, what happened then…?' But just when I think he might leave me to *chillax*, he goes and sits—on my bed, if you don't mind. 'Earlier, in the sitting room?'

'Oh, it was nothing—just a bit of old-fashioned homophobic bullying.'

He frowns, like he doesn't comprehend. Maybe it's true then: the chickens are no longer getting the shit kicked out of them in their playpens. 'You don't think…?'

'What?'

'Well, the boss thinks you may have been winding Harold up.'

'Ah.' And she's sent her little *fag* up.

'So, you weren't then?' He gives me a side-glance.

'I was just being who I am.' Side-glances and snickers: that's all I've had since the moment I walked in here. 'It can be provocation enough sometimes.'

'Give it time, Joan.' He pats my knee. 'They'll come round eventually.'

'Darling.' I knock his hand away. 'I've spent a lifetime waiting for the world to catch up. But time is a luxury I no longer have.'

He shrugs, stands. 'Well, you seem to have made one friend.'

I shake my head at him. 'All my friends are long in the ground.'

It is not entirely true—Gladys being an exception to this rule—and my delivery is throwaway; nevertheless, my words land with some gravity. He frowns, words forming on his tongue; then he seems to change his mind about them. 'Nice ribbons.'

He is smiling; my smile in return is condescending. But as he is withdrawing, with a wiggle of his bottom, I find myself conceding that perhaps—in here—that poor woman *is* the closest I have to a friend. She took my side against the rest of them. And you take what you can.

Once upon a time, I would have *taken home* that one, closing the door behind him. My dear, once upon a time he would have been paying! Which reminds me—must ring the oldest call girl in the book. *Have I rung Gladys yet?* She said she'd come visit. Now that'll set the cat among the pigeons. As I head out to the

41

balcony, I'm almost chuckling.

It's not quite a crescent moon, more a quarter—waxing or waning, I'm not sure. Some stars, stitched here and there. Of course, that's how it began. Running up a few sequins. *Love what you're wearing—could I have one in midnight with batwings? Certainly sir, would that be small or medium?* Then I started making some bits for the West End. Earnt a bob or two. As the shows got bigger, the costumes and the cheques followed suit. Next thing, I'm at the Royal Opera. Back then, a boy from Hackney could still climb the social strata.

I'm so *away with the fairies*, I don't hear his door opening; I do hear him coughing.

'Oh look, it's neighbourhood watch.' I barely glance in Jim-Jam's direction.

'I must ask you to please extinguish that.' There it is again—the clipped consternation of a baritone Kenneth Williams.

I carry on smoking. 'What ya gonna do, big man? Raise the alarm again?'

He clenches his fists, all shrivelled and powerless.

'Well, go on then.'

Most of the world's problems could be solved by eliminating *little men*. And other big discussions we had *back then*. But still the show is run by them.

'I am… simply concerned for your well-being.'

Oh, pull the other one. 'If you were really concerned for my well-being, you might have made yourself known in the sitting room this morning.'

He rises to his full five foot seven.

'I think you know what I'm saying.'

And suddenly he's squaring up to me across the abyss between our balconies. *I mean, really.*

'Who the hell do you think you are? Flouncing in here with all your…'

'You're not one of them.' My gaydar is rarely wrong.

He is guilty by hesitation. 'I don't know what you mean.'

To drive the point home, I break into song. '2-4-6-8. Gay is just as good as straight.'

His eyes widen in horror.

I sing louder. '2-4-6-8! Gay is just as good as straight!'

His eyes widen further. 'Stop it. They'll hear.'

The blender-inners never want to be discovered. Too late for that, *my dear*. Below, a quadrangle of light appears.

I add some moves as I crescendo to climax, my joint tip a glow stick. '2-4-6-8!! Gay is just as good as straight!!'

'Stop!' Jim-Jam all but yells.

And I do. His loss of control yielding an unexpected thrill.

Below a shadow fills the quadrangle. A key rattles.

'Always the same, you lot.' Jim-Jam bares his dentures. 'Shouting from the rooftops and spoiling it for the rest of us.'

'Oh, fuck off! You and all the other apologists. You're worse than the fucking straights.' I fling the remains of my joint to the garden as the back door opens, leave him to brazen the care assistant. And battle his conscience: even by the light of a quarter-moon, I can see I have wounded him.

2-1.

Jim

His tie is neatly knotted. His hair is neatly parted. His eyes he avoids and turns to face the door. In one hand, his briefcase—leather, lightly scuffed—in the other, his cane—walnut, with comfort grip; everything is set.

With a ping, the lift reaches its destination. Its doors slide across his field of vision with the pleasing precision of a ruler across a drawing.

The layout before him is not the one he has been modelling in his head. Instead of an office—open-plan, panoramic—there is a sitting room, cluttered and cramped. Its walls are not the Nordic neutral which makes his heart sing; they are a noxious green. In fact, the design is *all* wrong. The chairs are wingback, not ergonomic—their occupants slumped, static.

He must have pressed the wrong button. He looks down at the control panel in confusion. There are only two levels: the one he is on and the one he has come from.

'You okay Jim?'

He looks up to see a woman. She is young; Southeast Asian, Jim assumes. She is wearing a uniform and plastic apron. He remembers where he is, and why he is there.

'Jim?' She takes his arm.

He hesitates, whispers. 'Have you seen Joan?'

She guides him from the lift and towards the garden—its door open, as if awaiting. He is aware of someone watching him: that woman. Eileen. She steals her eyes away as soon as Jim catches them. When he catches the sound of typewriters tapping, he is shaken all over again.

'Maybe you need sit down?' The woman in the apron tightens her hand.

The sound is needles, knitting: the woman in the dressing gown, her booties now almost fully-formed.

'What he needs is someone to look after him.' Eileen is now smiling a gap-toothed grin. 'A woman's touch, if you know what I mean.'

Swiftly, Jim shrugs away the woman-in-apron. 'I'm fine.' He steers himself across the doorstep, and into the garden.

It reminds him of his own; it must be getting overgrown. He must get back there soon. But first, there is something that must be done: first, he must face up to Joan.

Joan is at the bottom of the garden—face a satellite dish, receiving the sun. He does not see Jim. He does not see the curlicue his smoke is inscribing in the sunshine. His eyes are shut. They open on hearing Jim forcing one foot before the other one. He looks Jim up and down. 'I think you'll find smoking *is* permitted in the rose garden.' His voice is a gauntlet thrown.

Jim stops, stands ground. Joan puts out his cigarette without finishing it and makes to move past him. Jim has to say something; it is not the line he has been rehearsing. 'Did you ever visit the Regent's Park rose garden?'

Joan pauses, pockets the cigarette stub.

Jim fears it may not be fully extinguished: the faux-fur of Joan's jacket looks somewhat hazardous.

'*Queen Mary's?*' Joan takes care to extract every available syllable of innuendo.

Jim takes a sudden interest in Joan's footwear. 'And there's another, in Hyde Park.'

'That's right—I used to cruise there at night.' Joan's comeback is as shocking as the pink of his Birkenstocks.

45

'I...' Jim finds words failing him.

Joan sets his head at a sixty-degree incline.

'I...' *I'm sorry*, Jim wants to tell him. *I should have said something. I've been a bridge in suspension between evening and morning, between the compression and tension of loneliness and deception, the do I or don't I of revelation.*

Between Joan's brows, a parabola is forming.

'I...' *I've sat all night unsleeping with your words spinning, the torque and friction of fear and self-loathing keeping them going.* But now—in daylight, in the garden—their momentum is decreasing, and he is a top toppling, soft-side showing. He hears himself saying, 'Richard always loved roses.' And what he means is—*you were right about me, by the way.*

Joan is smiling, just a smidgen; Jim knows this means they have an *understanding*.

The garden had been Dickie's domain. He'd looked after everything at home, made it nice for them. Jim had always been busy, working. Jim has always been busy with something. Indeed, he has never found time to explore *this* garden before. Though, in truth, there is not much to be discovered—some desultory planting, a patch of patchy green. Even at their modest pace, it doesn't take long to cover its corners. Or, it seems, the common ground between himself and Joan.

'So, um...' Jim prods again at the embers of their conversation. 'What brings you here, then?'

'Danger unto myself. Or so they tell me.' Joan flicks a hand, as if swatting ashes away. 'And I neglected to deposit any progeny by way of insurance policy.'

'You don't have *any* family?'

'It's been some decades since they wanted anything to do with me.'

'I'm sorry.'

'Don't be.'

Jim has one niece. They are down to Christmases and consolations. The last card Jim can remember receiving was when... her mother, Jim's sister, had also passed away.

'And what brings you here, young man?' Joan steals a sideways glance at him.

'Oh, I shan't be here long. Just until I find a position.'

'A position?' Joan's brows arch for the boughs above them.

'Then I'll be going home.'

'I see.' Joan's face forms that expression, the one they all give him—like they don't believe him.

Circuit complete, they repeat. As they pass the open door to the sitting room, Jim is again aware of that woman—Eileen—watching them as avidly as her usual morning television. Her face is affronted as a seagull, salvaged fish supper snatched from its beak. His step falters a moment. 'Please don't tell anyone.'

'That you're leaving?'

'That I'm...'

'A dirty little queer?'

Jim feels shame surge across his skin to hear those words again: in his body, he carries a chronology of times they have been spoken of him—openly in games changing rooms, under breath on a stygian crossing when that handsome Egyptian ferryman had caught him looking.

Joan looks him up and down with what can only be described as disappointment, his lip curling. 'Your secret's safe with me, dear.' He keeps walking.

Jim follows, silently contemplating. When he had found himself in this—he will not use the word *home*—in this place, he found certain assumptions had been made about him. He had not seen occasion to challenge them. Assumptions had often been made about his 'wife' at home. His mother had gone to her grave believing Dickie lodged in the spare room. Of course, close friends had known. Dickie had been a touch younger than Jim, and a touch more open; in time, chosen colleagues had also known. Dickie had attended the requisite functions and proved himself popular amongst them. He always was a charmer. A talker. At dinners, Jim would happily sit silent for hours as Dickie gabbled about something or other. How hollow the house had sounded with his voice no longer in it.

And how huge this small square of green seems as they lap it a third time, neither of them saying anything, and only as they are once more approaching the door to the living room does another question burn its way to the tip of Jim's tongue. 'So why Joan?'

'Why not?' Joan veers towards the only bench in the garden.

Jim is uncertain if he is to join. But could do with a sit down. Really, he must get in shape again soon. When he gets home. Because home he shall go, whether they believe him or no.

'Ah…' An involuntary exclamation escapes Jim as bench meets bottom. Joan does not acknowledge him—sits hands in lap, knotting and unknotting his digits. 'Your rings…' Jim's eyes are drawn to them, sparkling in sunshine. 'You have so many of them.'

Joan pounces a hand in the air, as a cat might its paw. 'You like 'em? You paid for 'em!'

It is a reference Jim does not understand.

'Liberace.' Joan turns then, looks Jim down and up. 'Another closet.'

Jim averts his eyes from rings now knuckle-dusters on closing fingers, wishing he'd not bothered. In the sky, a solitary bird.

'You don't have any yourself?' The question is innocuous enough, but Joan's tone uppercuts.

Jim shakes his head, keeps watch overhead.

'Not even the one?'

Of course, they would have done. Without question. Given the legislation. 'He died.' But the bill had still been pussyfooting through parliament.

Joan's tone softens, slightly. 'I'm sorry.'

'We never had the opportunity.'

It must have been... Two thousand and three? Four? The years blur. But it was shortly after Jim had taken early retirement on a comfortable pension that Dickie started experiencing some discomfort in his abdomen. By the time the diagnosis was confirmed, it had spread to other organs.

Jim deflects attention from these reflections. 'Did you have a partner?'

Joan guffaws. 'No-one in particular.'

As they sit silent beside each other, Jim's mind inevitably wanders—to funerals, to flowers. Dickie had been well-loved: the service was well-attended, the wreaths glorious. And then they lay in the conservatory, withering; then Jim had come home and it had been just him, when he had been so looking forward to it being just the two of them. Dickie had always been the one who made social engagements. Without him, Jim couldn't see the point in them. At first, a few friends had rung to check on him. But in the absence of the necessary reciprocity, they also withered away.

'Lunchtime!' Joan pulls him back to the present again, points out the woman-in-apron: she is waving them in.

Jim usually has a good breakfast to set him up for the day; this morning, he'd not been hungry. Now he notices his stomach rumbling. 'Let's just hope it's not jerk chicken.'

'Oh, I'm rather fond of jerking.' Joan jumps on the line, as though fed him by a *straight man*. 'And chickens.'

A sudden smile slips between them.

After lunch—today a passably palatable macaroni cheese—there are always *activities*, helicoptered in like a birthday party entertainer to a child who would really rather *Jack Horner* in a corner. That afternoon is *games*. Not hockey, rugby, cricket. But Monopoly, Scrabble, chess. Jim would never usually join the 'fun'. But the morning's conversations have brought so much back to him that his head is too full to fit anything else in. He puts his book down, checks who's looking. Across the sitting room, Eileen and the Jamaican-Nigerian gentleman are heads down over backgammon; Jim is not sure he has seen them play together before. The coast is clear: he can accept Joan's invitation to join him in a card-game.

'Snap!' It is not the one he would have chosen. And his exclamation is louder than the one he'd been expecting; he has laid down a matching sovereign.

Joan thinks this hilarious; no longer empty-stomached, perhaps, he has shed the morning's surliness. 'Two old queens, look!'

And everyone *is* looking. Jim is conscious that his standing amongst the other residents has shifted. Joan does not need to say anything: Jim is damned by association. In their eyes, he is now 'batting for the other team'. Eileen's look, from the opposite end of the coffee table, suggests she wouldn't now use a barge pole to touch him across the length of its imitation grain. He hangs his head and hauls the cards in.

'You know you mustn't mind them.' Joan is waving like an actual queen. 'When you start minding them, they're winning.

That's where Wilde went wrong.'

It isn't just Joan's clothing that requires a hazard warning: it is his entire person. 'And you.' Jim finds himself returning fire at him. 'With the… Jamaican gentleman, yesterday afternoon.'

'I believe he's Nigerian.' Joan shoots back, quick as anything.

Glancing up, Jim sees Eileen and the gentleman in question have returned to their dice in indignation. But the woman-with-knitting is waving back at Joan. So now there are three on their team. Imagine, all this time—however long it is Jim has been sitting in this room—he could have had a friend in this woman. Dickie would have made it the work of seconds—in this, at least, he was not unlike Joan—who is now blowing a kiss across the room. The woman receives it, smiling—like a last rite, or first valentine.

'Another game?' Jim starts shuffling.

'Strip poker this time?' Joan is almost flirting.

As a child, Jim spent hours puzzling over jigsaws, building Meccano empires. He has forgotten the pleasures of playing, of losing oneself in something. A curious contentment comes over him; he barely notices the hours passing. Suddenly, it is evening. And Joan is sighing. 'Who do you have to fuck to get a drink round here?'

They are now collaborating on a game of Patience and have fallen into a rhythm. Jim lays a card down. 'I was never much of a drinker.'

'I pickled my liver.' Joan lines up another. 'Smoked my lungs—all my organs are in deadly competition.'

'You shouldn't say such things.' For Jim they are too close to bone.

They are almost alone in the sitting room. The others have already turned in. Except the woman-with-knitting. Her hands are resting against the quilting of her dressing gown, head slumping. With evening comes the changing of the guard, and the man-in-uniform is now tidying around her. When he glances over, Jim shifts in his seat, self-conscious again. He looks back to their cards, sees what Joan has done. 'You can't put a king on top of a queen.'

'Oh, I never paid much mind to that top-bottom thing.'

It is not entirely true to say Dickie had done *all* the talking at dinner parties: though sparing with it, Jim had been known for his *demi-sec* wit. And when he nudges Joan, nods to the man bending to retrieve something, blood drips again into desiccated veins. 'Now there's a lovely bottom.'

Joan slaps Jim, playfully on the arm. 'Hands off bitch, he's mine.'

The man-in-uniform stands, booties in hand; he is frowning, focuses his frown on them. 'And what have you two got to giggle about?'

Joan rests his cheeks in his hands, eyelashes oscillating. 'Nothing.'

In his own cheeks, Jim feels blood rising.

'Go on. Pack up now, it's bedtime.' The man-in-uniform has turned stern again.

They swiftly vacate the sitting room, take the elevator up to their own rooms. And before Jim knows it, Joan is key in, casually waving. 'Night.'

'Night then.' As his own door shuts behind him, Jim sets about unpacking what has befallen—such a day it's been. The most eventful in... well, since he can't remember when. His throat is sore from so much speaking, but this is not his strangest feeling; in his belly there is an aching. Perhaps his acid reflux returning; or perhaps, as lemon juice reveals the papercut that one was previously unaware of, a squeeze of social interaction has revealed to him the seclusion of his current situation. The fact that he can hear muted movement next door only makes the silence seem deeper. He finds himself almost hoping for a little night-music to fill it. He has heard nothing since his protestation the other evening. It now makes him sad to think he has deprived Joan of something which brings some comfort to him.

Jim's evening routine is, for him, comforting—dressing gown on, watch off, book open. He doesn't believe he has any intention of reading: it is the photograph that's calling him. It was taken the summer of his retirement. They had treated themselves to a tour of the Highlands. Or was it Lowlands? There had been mountains. And they had both been rather taken by them—those divine greens and auburns. They'd even discussed relocating.

In this picture, Dickie is wearing a jumper purchased from a woollen mill they stopped in. In fact, they had each purchased one—Jim's grey, Dickie's blue—the fabric echoing his eyes, smiling into camera and into Jim's across the years.

There is a knock at the door. Jim closes his book on its marker. 'Come in!'

The man-in-uniform enters, with his usual pills but without his usual joie-de-vivre. 'Sorry I'm late. There's been an incident.'

'Ah.' Jim has been here before.

The man-in-uniform hesitates, out of respect. 'Mary.'

Jim struggles to put a face to the name as he swallows his pills down. The man-in-uniform mimes knitting; Jim understands then. *Poor woman.* How brief their triumvirate had been; now there are just two on their team.

He feels his arm patted, in a way which might be described

as manly. 'I'm sorry.'

Jim hands the pill cups back. 'Don't suppose there was anything you could have done about it.' He absolves the man of any further need to comfort him.

On his way out, the man-in-uniform pauses a moment. 'Didn't fancy Eileen, then?' And he gives Jim a smile—perhaps of consolation, perhaps of acknowledgement. 'Glad to see you're making friends.'

Craig. That's his name. Jim hears him rattle down the corridor, knock at Joan's door, but thereafter can hear nothing distinctly. Jim suspects his neighbour may take news of the poor woman's passing somewhat less stoically: he sees chinks in that armoury. He goes to wait on the balcony, hands rigidly resting against its chipped enamelled railing.

This too is something he has not allowed himself to do: always occupied, he never simply stands, looking. Of course, there is not much to see at this time. In the darkness, it is all so much blurring. But he can feel the air cooling, coming on to rain. He can hear the leaves rustling. And the breeze bears that *glorious* scent to him.

Dickie really had loved roses. He was always pruning, and planting new varieties with ludicrous literary names. *Silas Marner. Ancient Mariner.* Red, pink, orange. Yellow as wool. And it'd been something like a second death to see that to which Dickie had given life slowly fall away. Jim had tried his best to keep things up but—like social etiquette—he'd no real aptitude for it. And the truth is, the garden had gone to ruin long before Jim had had to leave it.

'Have you heard?' Joan's stage-whisper surprises Jim: lost in recollection, he had not heard the door opening.

Jim nods assent and, when Joan sparks up, doesn't dare

dissent: even in the lighter's brief flare, he can see his suspicions have been proved correct: beneath those scales, a soft-spot.

'I can't believe it.' Joan's hands are a blur of smoke and mirrors. 'I mean, we just saw her. It can only have been an hour...'

'It's a long time in here.'

'But surely someone should have noticed something was wrong?'

Jim had not noticed anything wrong: in that picture, taken in Scottish sunshine, the tumour was already growing.

'I should have noticed. I could have done something...' Joan's voice is straining.

'I don't think...'

'She died alone while we sat watching!'

'We all die alone, Joan.'

Actually, Jim had been in the room—holding Dickie's hand. But the poor thing was so far gone on morphine, Jim doubts he even noticed him.

'Oh, how awful.' And Joan's melodramatics are suddenly gone as he weighs the stark facts in the still of his palm.

The light and Jim's vision are too dim for him to see clearly but he suspects his new neighbour, friend possibly, is having 'a good cry'. And perhaps Jim might even have pressed that palm in his own, brought some comfort to Joan, were they not on separate balconies. Or at least patted his shoulder manfully. But all he can do is say, 'I'm sorry.'

Joan inhales, exhales. The rain starts to fall. And then after a while, Joan says with a voice which suggests a sad smile, 'Now she'll never know if it's a boy or a girl.'

Joan

Today I am grey as the sky, as grey as I sometimes find my memory.

I used to use an old-school haberdasher at the far end of the Portobella. Of course, it's no longer there. Run by a veteran transwoman. Of course, I can't remember her name. How I loved it. Complete chaos. Colour! Texture! Bows, beads, buttons everywhere. I would look around and think, *well this is a trip—it's like the inside of my head.*

Now my mind is a candle, long-melted. And my memories moth wings caught in it: I'm so absorbed in unsealing one from its wax—Michael, or Martin perhaps—that I do not mind my step.

'Careful!' Jim hesitates a hand.

I stop myself from falling flat on my face and—to recover it—make like the whole thing is happening to some other dizzy queen. 'Can't even walk straight, that one. Not since she had the stroke that time.'

I was fifty-seven. Which seemed young for it to happen. But then, after a lifetime burning both ends, it was hardly surprising. I had to learn to take things easier, *imagine*. And learning to wield scissors again was quite the challenge. One I rose to, with aplomb. But if I'm honest, my pattern cutting was never quite the same. One side still works less well than the other.

Jim's hand returns to *his* side again. 'I would never have known.'

He's a stuffy old stick, but a gentleman. And, with Mary Magdalene gone, the closest I have to a friend in current environs.

'Would it work better if we swap around?'

I've always been *on the left* of the spectrum, but there's a first time for everything: we change positions and carry on perambulating the 'lawn', its grass glistening treacherously with yesterday's rain. I try to watch where I'm walking, stop my thoughts straying, but something has been set off by that poor woman's passing.

I hardly knew her. Yet at breakfast—sat beside her empty chair, hearing those hushed conversations I can't bear, about how she's now *up there*—well, I couldn't even finish my cuppa—I mean, it's not as if whatever his name is—begins with an 'H'—it's not as if his holiness ever had time of day for her. So it was either an altercation over the All-Bran, or get out to the garden. And I was pleased, secretly, when Jiminy Cricket came to join me. Today, I need company—dear me, not *that* sort of company—a *companionable silence* is the technical term, I believe.

What I'm finding troubling is the feeling I might have *done* something. I've always been a man of action. *Direct action!* That's what we were about back then. But who am I kidding? What could I have done? She was about a hundred and one. All those young men, dying one by one—I could never do anything for them.

Jim nudges my arm and I'm back in the garden. It u-bends around the rear of the building and we can go no further in this direction. He is nodding to something through the fencing. Like cooped chickens given a glimpse of freedom, we can see the driveway out front. There are two cars parked there—one big black one and one other. The undertaker and our Dear Departed's daughter. The teabag-lady had *heard* they were both here—relayed it across the toast rack like the best society gossip. *Eileen.* That's it. As in *Come On.* As in *my tits.* (On which she so regularly gets.)

We're about to return the way we came, when what must be Mary comes into view around the corner—in an all-in-one number, born aloft like Marilyn or Madonna. The pallbearers slip her out the side door—just the other side of the fencing from where we are—open their back door, slide her in like a pizza, and she's off to *meet her maker*. Then we hear the front door, and two women appear—one with grey hair, the other a brunette. Even at this distance, even I can see she's pregnant. She slides into the passenger seat and is about to shut the door when a final figure runs towards her, hijab flapping. In Madam's hand—sharp in the sunshine, which breaks through the cloud just at that moment—is something lemon. And when she hands the younger woman the booties, my floodgates open. 'I hope she likes the ribbons.'

I feel Jim's hand on my arm, still and calm; as I said, a gentleman.

I turn to him. 'Honestly, that one. She'll weep at the drop of a hat pin.'

And somewhere, a large lady sings; she continues warbling as we carry on walking, talking—the release of tears appears to have also released my tongue. 'So what sort of position would you want to be taking, if you don't mind me asking?'

'At this point, I'd take anything.'

'Anything?' I raise my intonation.

He lowers himself to laughing. 'Preferably in the field of Civil Engineering.'

I've no idea, *I'm certain*. 'So what's one of them do, then?'

'Well, we build things.'

'What sort of things?'

'Civic infrastructure. Roads, railways, bridges…'

'I've chained myself to a few of those.' I arch one eyebrow higher than the other.

Jim's knits his together. 'To what end?'

'Civil disobedience is more my line: I'm in the business of bringing things down.'

'What sort of things?'

'Clauses. Ages of Consent. Capitalism.'

'You've got your work cut out for you, then.'

He's not wrong. And he's not a bad talker, as it happens—we keep on passing the time of day as we pass back into the sitting room, back and forth to the dining room, Eileen watching, whispering to the auditorium. 'And I could barely get two words from him.'

When evening comes and we find ourselves at the doors to our rooms, I find myself flirting beneath the foul-smelling floral arrangement framed between them. 'I don't suppose I could interest you in my record collection?' Goodness knows where it comes from, but it feels good to get these old ventricles pumping.

Jim looks like I asked him to donate an organ; he still isn't sure if he's coming or going as I'm pushing my door open and the lift is pinging and there, zimmer-framed, is Harold. As in *Wilson.* As in *Mary.* (Which he is not, quite clearly.)

'Evening!' I wave to him. He stands open-mouthed so long that the doors close again before he's even begun dismounting; it is a quite delicious moment.

Jim is still blushing as I shut the door behind him. 'You weren't joking.' He indicates the record collection, piled in the one and only chair. If I had known I might have a visitor, I *might* have tidied earlier. It is somewhat disordered in here—I'm still struggling to find a home for everything, and there's clothing simply everywhere—but, *alas*, no dirty knickers.

'Why else do you think I invited you in?' I simper à la Fenella Fielding. 'Sit down.' I gather the vinyl in my good hand. 'Would you mind terribly if I slipped something on?'

Really, I should have done *Carry On.*

'Be my guest.' Jim looks sheepish and sits, trousers rising up his legs. I notice again—socks and tie matching. The colour-coordinated ones are always absolute filth in the bedroom.

'Is that?' He's spotted the photo on the bedside cabinet.

'It is.'

He looks at me and then at the picture again, as if to say *what happened?*

I try to conjure something witty, woven with *Dorian Gray.* But it doesn't come, so I deflect attention to the matter in hand. 'Something atmospheric… Shostakovich?'

Jim folds his coat over the arm of the chair with the precision of a confirmed engineer. 'I know nothing about opera.'

'You know I worked there?'

'As a singer?'

'As a costume maker.'

'Ah.' He has a lightbulb moment, looking at the tangerine chiffon I've draped over their dreadful light-fitting. 'So that's where you got all yours, then?'

I make my selection. 'Darling, those aren't costumes.' Take the liner from its cover, vinyl from its paper. 'If they were, I'd be playing a part.' I lower my voice as I lower record onto spindle, lower the needle. 'Which I am not.' And up rises that wonderful opening glissando.

Jim fidgets in his seat. *Perhaps I left a pea beneath it?*

Or perhaps his discomfort is something to do with my uncharacteristic overemphasis…

Oh well. In for a cent, in for a euro. 'Don't suppose you can roll?' And as Ms Popp casts a spell with her mellifluous soprano, I magic my stash from my handbag—*ta dah!*

He looks like I asked him to donate both kidney and liver.

Oh dear. I settle for the bed, as he has the chair. 'So, what did you wear?' I start to assemble a bifter. 'As a civil servant?' I go full Diana-doe-eyes on him. 'Or were you a naked one?'

'I was a clothed one,' he says with sudden strictness; it is almost erotic. 'In sensible shoes and a sensible suit with a sensible haircut and a sensible life. And really you must find me terribly tiresome and it's time for me to go.' He begins rising; at our great age, sometimes nothing could be harder than simply standing up or sitting down: one can get stuck in one position.

'Where? Home?'

He hovers, semi-erect.

'Do you really believe that?'

The cruelty of this question becomes apparent the moment it is spoken: it's probably the only thing keeping him going, the illusion that one day he *will* return home. I attempt an alternative position. 'This song… It's by Dvořák. It's about the moon. How he travels around the world and looks into homes.' The stage is for illusions. Life is for *solutions.* 'Shall we see if he's looking into this one?'

I've always found a smoke solves most things. I know; I shouldn't: I have promised *Miss Thing* I wouldn't: Craig. As in *David.* As in *Goliath.* (Which is how I like to imagine his appendage.) Apparently, Madam is *on to it.* Apparently, she recognised my particular shade of lipstick and is limbering-up to bring Social Services down on me since she found a butt beneath my balcony.

It's tight for two, I must say. Still, Jim keeps to his side of the Juliet as I light up, shrugging. 'Rules are there to be broken.'

The moon is having a good old gander. Half-smile like the Mona Lisa. *I see what you're up to down there.* He's seen better:

61

waving, white, on the water, when I went double-dipping with Paul—or was it Peter? I clearly remember what we were doing *down under*.

'A little chink in the wall between us?' I offer Jim the joint, test *his* water.

Now it's lung, liver and kidney. 'No, I…'

'Oh, learn to live before you die.'

Again I realise, belatedly, it is not a kind thing to say—what with his partner having passed away. I think I see tears as he turns his face from me. And I'm framing some form of apology when he turns back again, like some gear has shifted inside of him. Then, well I never, he reaches out and takes the gear from my hand. Holds it between thumb and fingertip like it might detonate any minute. Surveys the scene—always concerned who could be looking—and sucks on it, like a straw in thick milkshake.

I hold my breath, wait.

He coughs, inevitably, splutters, uncontrollably.

I laugh, loudly. 'Let me give you a blowback.'

'A what?'

It's like I'm back behind the bike sheds. Though that was mostly blow*jobs*. I get him in position—stiff as a board, this one—then assume my own. Space invaded, he makes to withdraw. I hold him there, a hand to shoulder. We are close enough to smell each other—he is halitosis and I, body odour.

He blinks in terror. 'Are you sure this will work?'

'Just breath in as I breath out.'

I purse my lips around the lit tip; his are around the other end, which is traced by lipstick. And I'm staring straight into his widened eyes. It's hard to tell in this light, but they are not brown. Or blue, even. They are an unexpected green.

There is nothing wrong with my close vision, and as I breath out and he breathes in, as time holds its breath a moment, I see something *in* his eyes I also was not expecting; something I've not seen in some time.

Attraction.

The moment is shattered in a spray of spit. *I usually charge extra for that.* I cannot stop the joint tumbling, my reflexes too slow. As I pat Jim on the back, I notice the quadrangle of light below. And the retreating shadow.

Uh-oh.

'Well, that's blown some cobwebs out!' Jim is giggling; I gallows humour him, say nothing. 'Well, blow me down!' That one little puff has gone straight through him, and I seem to be hallucinating: there are no alarms, no bolts of lightning. 'Well, that's struck a blow for...' But then a knock on the door interrupts his laughter and Jim goes up a gear to paranoia. I raise a hand to reassure—*I have been here before*—and usher him into the room without speaking, as the knock comes again.

'Oh yes?'

The door opens. Craig stands silhouetted in the doorframe. From the tension in his outline, I can tell that the shadow glimpsed down on the lawn had not been a figment of my imagination.

Nevertheless, I stick a smile on it. 'I'm afraid you'll have to make your own introductions. You know I'm simply terrible with names.'

He doesn't even turn in my direction. 'I'm disappointed in you, Jim.'

I hand Jim's coat to him. 'Darling, you were just leaving.' This is my battle to lose or win.

Jim just stands, stoned and stunned.

Craig stands aside, nods permission. 'Should steer clear of

this one. Bad influence.'

'Please don't tell anyone.' Jim edges edgily past him. 'If I get a conviction, I'll never work again.'

There is some perversity in me which kicks in at the most inappropriate moments—operatic death scenes, in the crematorium when the coffin goes through the curtain. It happens again—I burst out laughing.

Jim is now fifth-gear. 'Perhaps it doesn't matter for a career in the theatre.' The value judgement is in the inflection. 'But if one is a Senior Engineer…'

For an engineer, he has a surprising understanding of the *linear*: Craig has to guide him through the door.

'Oh, now I'll never get out of here.' Jim disappears, muttering, down the corridor.

Craig shuts the door behind him. We are alone. And although I will not let it show, I feel suddenly vulnerable. Somewhat fearful. Of course, we have been taught to *fear the black man*. And I've fought such stereotypes with brown brethren on many a frontline. But this time the lines have been drawn in such a way that he and I are on opposite sides of them.

He raises the pill cup he's holding, tendons tautening in his arm. 'Swap—your drugs for mine.'

My headshake is firm.

He raises his other hand towards me—fingers firm as promises, spread wide to receive. 'Those are the rules, Joan.'

When police tried to lay down the law, break us up with *such-and-such act*, we would instead *ACT UP* and lie down in the street. 'Rules are there to be broken.' My lying days are done but still I can *stand* firm: he will have to carry me to the police van.

'Those are the rules and you'll have to learn to live by them.'

Now his hand is clenching.

My exterior remains *Swan Lake* serene, but inside is arrhythmic as *Rite of Spring*.

'I lied for you, Joan. Told her we'd spoken. That I was certain you weren't smoking in your room. That probably some kids had broken into the garden... You promised to be discreet. Then I find another butt. I mean, what if she had found it? And thank fuck she didn't find you pushing drugs on one of our most vulnerable residents. I mean, poor Jim—he probably doesn't know what's hit him!'

He rattles the cup, quite out of time with the percussion section in my chest. My body starts shaking; my head shakes again.

He is teetering on the edge of another tantrum. 'Joan, my job is on the line.'

He's done his big number, so I shall do mine: *The Chosen One.* 'You know, in my day, the queers wanted to be different. You lot just want to fit in. We didn't want to get by in the world as it existed. We wanted to recreate it in our own image.' I turn from him with a final flourish.

'You obviously succeeded.' His hand is on my shoulder, his voice at my ear. 'How else would you have ended up in this place?'

'Kindly remove your hands from me.'

'Kindly give me your ganja!' He moves around to face me once more.

'Oh, fuck you and fuck your job—as if I care!'

This time, I have gone too far: this time, I have pulled the trigger.

He drops the cup at my feet. 'If you want your tablets, lick them off the carpet.' And his big finish: 'Knowing you, you'll probably enjoy it!'

I hold it, hold it; *never, ever let them see it...*

And only when the door shuts, do I collapse. I do not mean

to collapse—I have the hide of a rhinoceros, I do not show weakness—but my bones, my old bones, they just won't stand it—the bedposts and bedsheets, they just can't stop it—it's like I'm having that stroke again and I'm in slow motion and my mouth is open—a sound emerging—a piccolo giving its last gasp before that final thwack of the *Sacrificial Dance.*

And then, the curtain is falling. *I am not contorting on cream-coloured carpeting.* And then, and then, the curtain is rising. *I am not crawling on all fours to gather the pills that lay scattered.* And I am reborn, bouquet in hand. *I am not pressing a caplet to parched lips and struggling to swallow it in the hope, the hope, that it may do something to stop this.* For this thundering in my sternum is an audience applauding, rising to its feet.

For I shall never *ever* accept defeat.

Jim

A knock at the door. He will not answer. He knows who is there. Through the tissue-thin membrane between them, he has heard the latch opening, closing. Heard that uneven shuffle in the corridor.

He stands—book in one hand, photo in the other—willing himself not there. Though he knows disappearance is impossible in here: there is a peephole in every door, through which prisoners may be monitored. For a man who likes to keep himself to himself, this lack of proper privacy has been torture.

Another knock. That cough. 'Jim?' The nasal twang that penetrates everything.

That... *creature*. What had he given Jim? And what had possessed Jim to accept it from him? He'd not slept, his head a whirligig—scenes so vivid and so long undredged that they seemed to have happened to someone else. Scenes from his boyhood and from his manhood. Scenes which had stirred his blood. Those long nights of longing in the boarding school dormitory, on his island of bed sheets and springs, waiting for some warrior to venture across an ocean of opprobrium, to climb in and hold him; finally finding the bravery to make his own journey across that sea in those first furtive fumblings behind university cricket grounds, always with an eye through the trees lest somebody should see; those backward glances in big-city back-alleyways, and overdue ecstasies in overgrown cemeteries; those stolen intimacies after stealthy stair-climbs past the doorways of sharp-eared landladies; then that door of one's own to close, behind which consenting adults might do as they chose, and someone with whom to build a home.

In the centre of this vortex of remembrance, in the centre of night's darkness, he'd found the stillness, the whiteness of a double-page spread and as dawn began to outline the room, he began to draw up a plan.

He'd planned pipelines, power-systems, and perhaps the power to return had always been within him. He'd planned to be up before anyone, but *best laid schemes often go awry*. He must have nodded off, finally: the watch on his wrist tells him it is now time for breakfast. And as he hears those pink Birkenstocks limp off towards the lift, towards the dining room, he presumes, Jim allows himself to breathe again. And to think he'd entertained, under the influence yesterday evening, that there might be something between them.

In the morning's unflattering light, the notion is quite ludicrous; Jim is embarrassed. His loneliness has left him desperate; his desires have rendered him ridiculous.

'Old fool. No-one could replace you.' Looking down at the photograph, he feels the joy and the relief he'd experienced when his drawings had risen to beautiful, functional fruition. 'We're going home.'

He sets his beloved back in his book, his book in his briefcase, on the bed, neatly-packed. He seals his briefcase, picks it up. At the door, he balances the weight in his right hand with a suitcase in his left and looks around the room one last time. It is as if he had never been there.

He creeps the carpeted-corridor; breakfast time has worked in his favour: all the other residents appear to be downstairs. Normally, there might be a chorus of televisions clamouring from doors half-open; this morning, there is not one. Jim is a man too rational for religion, but today some god does seem to be smiling.

He does not take the elevator, but the stairs—the stairs that go to the side door used by cleaners and undertakers. There are more stairs than he has factored; his cases are heavier than he remembers: sweat starts to pour and his spectacles have slid almost past the end of his nose by the time he reaches the ground floor, where there is some sort of holding area for what appear to be miniature versions of the cranes he'd enjoyed watching, winching girders into position. Presumably these ones are for winching humans; he could have done with one to lift his damn luggage down.

With relief, he rests his cases on the floor, wipes his face with his coat sleeve, rights his glasses and—there it is—the world, framed by the door. And there he is, reflected in the glass of that door: he is a man of the world; he belongs there. He reaches for the push bar.

He presses down. Nothing happens.

He presses again and nothing happens.

He presses with both hands, pits all his weight against it. The bar remains rigid. *Can he really have become so weak, so pathetic?* No, it must be bolted.

He presses his forehead against the glass. His breath mists the pane; the world is slipping from view again. Jim is not a man much given to crying but his eyes are also misting. Everything is slipping.

No, that cannot happen. He must get away—away from that creature, away from all it might mean to *be* here. With the full force of his frustration and fear and love, he raises his fists and he strikes at the glass.

He strikes and he strikes, again and again. He's not sure what he'd been expecting. Not the sudden sine wave of a siren, piercing his cranium. Nor the sudden shot of pain, searing his veins. The blood dripping into his shirt cuff that he'll never get out again.

Dickie could always get a stain out of anything.

'Jim! What have you done?' The woman with the blue apron appears from one direction. It seems quite obvious what he has done: he has shattered a door-pane.

'Call the nurse, quickly.' The woman in the black head-covering appears from the other direction, and the first woman rushes out again. 'You really must stop this nonsense. I have already replaced that glass once.' The second woman shakes her head at him.

They all shake their heads at him. *Silly old man.* They take him to a room which smells of Savlon. A room which he has only once been in. That time they brought the doctor to see him. This time, they bandage his hand, bring tea with too much sugar in. And they look at him, these women, the way that woman on reception had looked at him on the day he'd reported, suited, to the office and she'd rung upstairs and one of the junior engineers, now silver-haired, had come down to tell him how *wonderful it was that he was there* and *would he like to take the tour* and *yes, these days everything's done by computer* and *no, they didn't have anything for him anymore* but perhaps *he could volunteer elsewhere* and *must dash* for some meeting or other but *don't be a stranger* and *there's the door.*

And now he is outside another door. And for some reason that creature, his neighbour is there. And for some reason his neighbour has a bandage in his hair. It does not appear to be a statement of fashion. They are sat side-by-side in a windowless corridor, waiting for something or other.

Joan. That is his name. A man called *Joan.* How... unusual.

Joan is first to break the silence. 'Joan and Jim went for a swim...'

And everything does seem to be swimming: when men are called Joan, there can be no fixed position. Another of last night's visions floats back to Jim: he had been home again—his childhood home, the nursery. He knows what he must say. 'To fetch a pail of water.'

'Ha!'

The illogicality of going for a swim to fetch a pail of water does not seem to matter: when men are called Joan, everything is up in the air. Jim keeps paddling. 'Joan *sank* down...'

'And broke his crown...'

'And Jim came *diving* after.'

To dive. To dive *in*. Without armbands. To feel molecules resisting and parting. To move beneath the surface of something. To see everything closer due to light's refraction: Joan seems more brittle, more broken, under close observation.

He turns his eyes from Jim's and throws them in the air. 'Must look a right pair.'

Then they hear the door. 'Right. Who is first?' It is the woman-in-black-head-covering again. And they are recalcitrant children, neither of them raising a hand.

'Jim!' She beckons. 'Joan and I have a *lot* to catch up on.'

Joan throws his eyes again. Jim catches them, isn't sure what to do with them. The woman-in-black takes hold of his arm, guides him. He does not like to be helped but it cannot be helped: for some reason his stick is not there, so he allows her to lead him away from Joan and through the door. He allows her to sit him in a chair.

He finds himself in some form of compacted chaos; he couldn't be certain if it is cupboard or office. There are papers on every surface, including the desk; the woman-in-black sits not *at* it, but *on* it. 'So...'

Jim finds her proximity unnerving.

'What seems to be the problem?' She is wearing something old-fashioned—rose or jasmine—and on her desk is an old-fashioned sign. Rashida Mirza.

Jim's first boss had one just like it, he remembers. Though she wasn't called Rashida. Ms something or other. Not Mrs or Miss. On that she was particular.

'It is not the first time this has happened...'

Jim looks down at his bandaged hand. He finds it hard to believe he could make such a mistake a first time, let alone repeat it.

'Jim?'

When he presses his good thumb against the bandaging, he finds clarity in the pain. He is seeing himself from the outside; he is cool, analytical: he is Jim.

'Look, I cannot just brush this under the carpet. You may forget why it was you came to us, but I am not able to do that.'

The search engine. Jim had been lost and it had found him.

'And neither am I able to help you, if you will not tell me what the problem is.'

A decline in functioning. That's what the doctor had diagnosed as the problem.

'Okay, let me hazard a guess...'

But Jim had declined to accept there could be anything wrong with his brilliant brain.

'Is it something to do with Joan?'

Just as Jim, it seems, has declined to accept other things. He looks up at her and frowns.

'Well, do not worry. I do not suppose he will be with us long anyway.'

He sees it then, with painful lucidity: sometimes we only know we want something when that thing is taken away. Like when he thought he'd outgrown the toys in his nursery—until he found himself in a boarding school dormitory. 'Why?' His thumb disengages from bandaging.

Ms Mirza seems reluctant to answer. 'Perhaps it is time to refer *you* elsewhere?'

Returned to the maze of his mind once more, Jim is immediately thrown by this detour. 'Where?'

'Another home.'

'My home?' It is as though a yellow brick road has been laid before him.

But her head is shaking. 'You are never going back there. It is time you accepted that, Jim.'

And his head is shaking, road map torn up again.

'When you came to us, you were in a state quite unfit to look after yourself and it was decided, in consultation with your closest relative...'

The woman, brunette, beside his hospital bed.

'...that a care home would be the best solution.'

What right had she to take that decision?

'I am sorry, Jim: your home is gone.'

What right had she to take his home from him? To take his hope from him? Again, he feels the world slipping. Again, he feels the fear and frustration rising within. And again, he feels himself crying.

But this time, the tears *do* bring release. Like somewhere inside, a bolt is shifting. Because if it is true, what she is saying—well then, he is free. From his own expectations. And from the fears and frustrations those expectations bring. And then that leaves only one thing.

She understands to leave him alone a moment, before laying a hand on his shoulder.

'I'm okay.' He nods his head, attempting to reassure both himself and her.

'You let it out, Jim. It is better.' She passes him a tissue from a box on the desk behind her. 'None of this stiff upper-lip nonsense. You let out the devil, and the devil has no power.'

He wipes his eyes, blows his nose; it's true, he does already feel a little improved.

'Now then, I do pride myself on running one of the more, shall we say, *caring* establishments in the area, and we should be sorry to see you leave here, but I am sure your niece would be happy to talk options over, if you feel you could be more comfortable elsewhere.'

'Is she here?'

'It has been some time since your niece was here, but if you would like to see her…?'

He shakes his head. 'I wouldn't want to trouble her.'

'You would not be any trouble, I am sure.' She pats him twice on the shoulder then, to indicate their meeting is over. 'And Jim, if you do decide you are staying, I do want that suitcase unpacking.'

His head is nodding again.

She helps him to stand. 'Shall I have someone help you to your room?'

'I'll be fine.'

She runs eyes over him, deems it safe to release him. 'Be a darling and send Joan in.'

Joan. The creature. The spinner. An unravelling thread that

could lead him from here. And there is Joan, in the corridor. Jim feels suddenly as light as an abseiler as he steps through the door.

'Steady.' Joan shoots out a hand.

With no stick to ground Jim, it seems everything is rocking. 'I'm fine.'

'And dandy?'

'Exactly.' A few steady breaths, and then it is just Jim's eyes that are rolling. 'Your turn.'

Only as he is about to turn the corner does Jim stop to wonder if Joan is *dandy*. What might be behind his mysterious headgear? But Joan has already disappeared behind Ms Mirza's door.

When Jim closes his own door, he finds his stick propped in the corner. He must have left it there this morning. And when he turns, he finds his cases returned before him. So many things are needing unpacking—feelings and possessions. It is like his body has made a decision, bypassed his brain: without thinking about what he is doing, Jim opens his briefcase, opens his book, pulls out the photograph. And props it on the bedside cabinet.

'What do you think, darling—could this be our home?'

Dickie, the homemaker: it is only right he should be here. He will always be part of Jim. And always be part of any room he should live in. Dickie had always brought the best out in Jim; perhaps, in being out in the open, he may do so again.

If Jim is, as they say, mislaying his marbles slowly, if he is a man prone to constructing his own reality then—really—what's to stop him from constructing it differently? If he has built a life on false foundations, then what is to stop him—with a lifetime's experience in engineering—from razing them and raising himself again?

He clicks his suitcase open. It would seem he doesn't have

much by way of building blocks with him. But on the dressing table, he sets up studio—with blank sheets and sharpened pencils. In the wardrobe, he suspends swatches—of ties and shirts and braces. On the bookshelf, he builds a library—of ancient aqueducts and modern masculinities. Vitruvius, *De Architectura. Who's a Pretty Boy, Then?* James Gardiner. When he steps back to survey his work, it is minimal, for sure. But Jim has always felt that less is more. There is no question he is now *here*.

He does not question his need to stretch roots further—follows a thread out the door, up the corridor, to the door of his neighbour.

He knocks. There is no answer.

He knocks again. 'Joan?' Answer there is none.

He is certain Joan cannot still be in Ms Mirza's room, sure he heard Joan's door slam earlier on. He thinks about peeping. But no: if Joan wants to be alone, Joan must be left alone. Though, perhaps he is in the sitting room. Or more likely, the garden. Smoking.

Jim follows his thread to the elevator. It pings before he gets there. The man with the nice bum steps from within, shakes his head at Jim. Jim remembers the man's disappointment, the last time he saw him. But now the man's voice is bright and loud; he has his music on. 'What *have* you done to your hand, young man?'

Jim frowns in confusion: he is not young. Though it's true he is feeling more youthful than he has in some time. He looks down at his hand, then up with conviction. 'It won't happen again.'

The man-with-nice-bum continues down the corridor. Jim all but hops into the elevator, watches the man—Craig, that's his name—knock hesitantly on Joan's door, and remove the contraptions from his ears. Jim thinks of calling *he's not there*, or, if he is, *he doesn't want to be disturbed*, but he is cut off by closing doors.

There is an *old man* in the mirror. An old man with bandaged hand and clothes all askew. And really, that won't do. That won't do at all. Jim straightens his tie and his collar, and is ready for the world once more.

The lift pings; Jim's thread leads him into the sitting room. There is a black and white film on the television. He knows, at the end, a woman gets on a plane. And a piano gets played, again. But he does not know its name. A black man and a white woman are watching. He does not know their names either. But he knows they are not who he is looking for.

He is led to the dining room. That woman, Eileen, is there with what must be her daughter, come to visit her. They are sipping tea from cups and saucers that only get used when guests are here.

'Hello there.' The daughter's eyes are like her mother's, only kinder. But she is not who Jim is looking for. As he turns and heads out the door, he hears Eileen whispering, and though he's certain it's something about him, he finds he is now past caring.

He returns to the living room, is tugged towards the garden. But the door is shut and there is no one to help him.

'What's wrong? Can't find your boyfriend?' It is the black man, the *Nigerian*. He has turned from the television and is talking to Jim.

Before caution can stop him, Jim is joking, 'Why? Do you fancy a threesome?' And it is like running—Dickie beside him, air singing past them, down the side of that mountain, as if it were never-ending.

77

The Nigerian trebles in size. 'Why, you bleeding...' He raises his fists at Jim.

And Jim finds his own fists raised back at him. And it is like he's in the playground, when his father had told him to *just show them you're a man and they won't call you names again,* but before the starting bell can ring, Ms Mirza strides in. 'Now, now boys.' Clapping her hands as if waking an army. 'I think we have had quite enough bleeding for one day.' And it turns out she is funny.

'Moffie man! He is moffie man!'

'Harold, I said enough!' And it turns out that she is on Jim's team.

Today, nothing is quite as it seemed. But true to expectation, the white woman—the one who never says anything—starts wailing.

'Now look what you have done.' Ms Mirza waggles a finger in Harold's direction.

Jim has never been called a *moffie man,* but suspects he is one and—far from being something of which he should be ashamed—he suspects it is the best thing about him. He puffs his chest so *Harold* can see it.

'Harold, we will not tolerate that sort of prejudice here.' Ms Mirza smiles at Eileen's daughter. 'I am *so* sorry, Clare. This is most unusual behaviour.'

Eileen's daughter, it seems, has come through to the sitting room in concern for Jim; she is smiling at him *because* he is a moffie man.

Jim smiles back at her, turns to Ms Mirza. 'Please may I go to the garden?'

'Of course you can, Jim.'

And then she is ostentatiously opening the door for him

and he is stepping into sunshine weaving its way through tree limbs, illuminating everything except the reason for his coming, which Jim cannot for the life of him…

Joan!

Joan is not in the garden. Joan is not even behind the rose bushes, smoking. Jim sees one of the bushes is broken. It looks like someone has fallen. Snapped stems. Bruised blooms. And hanging, limp as a wrist, one unblemished blossom.

Lemon.

Jim grasps it with his good hand, and he twists and he turns, taking care with the thorns. He frees the rose. He raises it to his nose. And he inhales. Right to the back of his nostrils.

It reminds him of soap on skin. And skin reminds him of so many things. Things which send his heart careening. Things he had forgotten. Things he will, heaven willing, take pleasure in knowing again with Joan.

Joan

I tap my heels together. One, two, three. Four. Before I even open my eyes, I can hear from the rustle of the duvet cover that I am still here. Polycotton. Easy-clean. There's no place like a home. And *this* home is no place for me. But in every place that ever seemed no home to me, I've refused to cut my cloth accordingly: it is the coat that must change, not me. I have stood defiant before parents, teachers, magistrates. I shall not stand to be humiliated.

But I shall not stand just yet. First, I must lay here for a bit. *Right side.* Check. *Left side.* Check. *Thank fuck.* That could have been it. *Little shit.* Just you wait.

I rise up from my mattress, plotting vengeance. Jury's out on weaponry. Customer dissatisfaction survey? Write to my MP? Or headline a red top—*PENSIONER FORCED TO EAT PILLS OFF CARPET.* Too sensational, even for me.

Gladys will have the answer. But Gladys isn't answering. Then, it is eight in the morning and she'll still be in her coffin. I leave a message and go knock on Jim.

Jim isn't answering. I peer through the peephole but it's all a blur and, of course, I've left my specs next door. I expect he's downstairs having soft-boiled and soldiers.

In the lift, I catch my reflection and wish I hadn't: I am still wearing yesterday's clothing, the clothing I (barely) slept in. I am the pig who didn't put lipstick on; I am a crab without exoskeleton as I scuttle across the sitting room. I hear conversation, and one word—uttered in Eileen's register— makes itself heard above all the others. 'Sick!'

As I round the corner into the dining room, the hush falling can mean only one thing: they have been talking. About me. Harold and Eileen. And Eugenia, in league. They all turn to look at me, guiltily.

'Morning!' My smile is a scimitar.

'You want toast?' The princess brandishes a butter knife in the air.

Jim is not there.

I change tactic. 'I'll just have a cigarette.'

'Well, that not very healthy, is it?'

'No, but then I'm sick. I mean, that's what you all think, isn't it?'

They do not deny it.

'Harold, could you please clear Joan's things? He will not be needing them.' Her highness sallies, frigid-shouldered, towards the kitchen, where they keep the cache of nicotine. I suppose they're thinking—if I have to keep asking—I'll get so sick of it I'll just stop smoking, but I shall show them.

'Well, best get moving.' Eileen pulls Harold's focus from Eugenia's receding bottom to the task in hand. 'Get ready for my visitation.' Between them they make a great show of clearing one bowl, one plate, one cup in matching melamine. 'I wonder if she'll bring her new man?'

'Has anyone seen Jim?' Neither of them will even look in my direction. And the woman who never says anything keeps chasing cornflakes around her bowl with a spoon, lifting them to her lips one by one.

'Thank you, Harold. Thank you, Eileen.' Princess Eugenia returns with a single Marlboro, and a rictus that could kill. 'You need lighter too?'

'Just open the fucking door, will you?'

As she stabs the code in and slings it open, you could

butter-cut the atmosphere. I moue and mince forth to take the morning air.

Usually I keep half back for later, but today I smoke the ciggy right down to the knuckles of my fingers as my mind seesaws.

Inhaling. *He's a cog in a system: it's not that young queen who needs reporting.*

Exhaling. *Why are you defending him? Not all gay guys are good guys. See Ernst Röhm. And Peter Mandelson.*

I am so preoccupied by my roundabouts and swings that I only slowly become aware of a siren, emerging from inside the building and echoing around the garden. And when I turn to see what's happening—I'm surprised to find Harold there, scowling.

'You keep a civil tongue.' He is blocking my path back into the dining room, fists clenching about his Zimmer frame. 'I'll not have you talk to the lady like that.'

'Oh really? And what are you going to do about it?' As I make to move past this great warrior in slippers, I see those fists rising, steel still clenched between them, feel steely pain in my shin and find myself moving in a direction quite different to the one I'd been intending. The sky is also in motion. Motion slow enough for cinematic flashback. ACT UP. 'Arresting' that bishop. Administered that right hook by one of his congregation. Then the cracking and crashing and yellow things circling like some children's cartoon. But now, instead of stars, they are blooms.

When I come round again, I am in some interrogatively-lit room and a series of busy bees are stinging me with salves, swaddling me in sympathy. Then bringing me before their Queen—headscarfed à la Audrey, but without the sunglasses.

She makes me wait in an airless corridor while she sees to my neighbour—who is also there, bizarrely bandaged from forearm to finger. I've no idea what's going on with him, I'm sure, but Madam Mirza appears to perform a personality transplant in the quarter hour he's with her—when he emerges from her office once more, I fear he may fall flat, so buoyant is his step. Perhaps she also replaced a hip.

By the time I enter her stuffy little lair, she is behind her desk, behind her screen, with the look of a surgeon who must announce an amputation. 'So, what happened in the garden? Your version.'

'Well, he attacked me with his Zimmer frame!'

Framed by frames I can only see the backsides of—but which will almost certainly contain the faces of all her laughing children—her face is cracking. 'I see.'

'I fail to see what's funny.' I have always failed to see humour in the pillory of another—from school dinner to city square.

She puts a lid on it. 'I am sorry.'

Too late: she's got beneath my bonnet. 'And *I* am not paying you however many hundreds and thousands for your hospitality to sit here and be insulted!' I rise from my seat.

'I believe your keep is being paid by his majesty's government.'

And there it is: the entitlement, the resentment. You see it everywhere: mothers with those monstrous pushchairs—*excuse me but I have more right to be here because I had a penis ejaculate in my vagina.* Grown-up kids with grown-old parents in wheelchairs—*excuse me but I have more right to be here because I helped build the Great Heteronormative Empire.*

'And you expect me to be grateful for that? I've paid my tax same as you straights have.'

'I am sure you have, Joan.' She remains studiously deadpan. 'And I shall be sure to have a word with the gentleman in question...'

'What exactly is your policy on LGBT residents?'

By the look on her face at that, and one might think I'd trod dogshit into the mosque carpet. 'Well, it is not something we have had to deal with before.'

'Are you sure?'

She tips an ear towards her shoulder. 'Are we talking about someone in particular?'

Now, I've been on a few public outings, back in the day of *Back to Basics*; politicians and priests deserved it. But not *vulnerable* old men; it's only himself Jim is hurting. 'No, we're talking about a point of principle. You have assumed that everyone who comes through your door is, like you, a nice little breeder.'

And then it is handbags at dawn. 'You are making something of an assumption there, Joan. For all you know, I may have *lost* all my children.' Her voice is broken by just a crack of emotion. 'Perhaps you might try to be a bit more broadminded yourself— and a little more tolerant of the rest of us?'

'I will not tolerate intolerance!'

'And I will not tolerate the consumption of an illegal substance.' She is coolly controlled again. 'Whilst you remain with us, you will please relinquish any such substance and refrain from smoking anywhere but the designated area. Should you find that problematic, I recommend the Smokefree service, freely available on the NHS.'

I am wounded but not defeated: I have one last shot in *my* handbag.

She picks up a pile of papers, taps them together. 'Now, is there anything else I can help you with?'

'Yes.'

Half-hour later, when I am back upstairs and the knock comes upon my door, I do not answer. It will be *him*, or it will be *her*.

'Joan?'

It is neither. But still I do not answer. I hear Jim's footsteps lilt off down the corridor. And I just lay there. Staring at the ceiling. I cannot even bring myself to put music on. The only sound is buzzing—a solitary fly spiralling in and out of vision. It too is trapped in here.

And then there's *another* knock at the door. I roll over to face the magnolia.

The knock comes again, firmer this time. And I hear the door opening. 'Room service.' It's him.

A whole colony of creepy-crawlies are now swarming. But I am rhino-skinned; I do not let them in. 'If you want your drugs, I suggest you get down and lick them off the carpet. Knowing you, you'll probably enjoy it.'

Let's see how this one likes the taste of his own medicine.

I do not catch what Craig says, beneath breath: I can hear nothing over the blood beating a *tarantella* in my ear. But I *feel* him drop to all fours—so emphatically that floor and bedstead tremor. Slowly, I roll over. Sneakily, peak across shoulder. I'm surprised by a sliver of bum-crack where his trousers have ridden down a bit; he is picking grey-green grass from the carpet upon which I've scattered it. *That'll show him, won't it.*

He turns and I turn away again. I hear him standing, shuffling; the speech is coming.

'Last night… My behaviour was inappropriate.'

'She tell you to say that?'

'She told me you made a complaint.'

'I did.' I confess it—I shot the deputy sheriff.

'I'm sorry, I…' Some silence, some throat-clearing. 'I had a bad day at home and…'

'You had a bad day!' I turn to face him and, as eager as I am to learn what can possibly be amiss with his perfect marital bliss, I'm not about to let him off the hook easily—not after how he's treated me. 'So you thought you'd take it out on a *vulnerable* elder entrusted to your care?'

'And I should not have done that.' His eyes are disarmingly candid. 'I said I'm sorry, Joan. I meant it.'

'You know, the trick to tearing up the rulebook is to not get caught doing it.'

He breaks eye-contact first. 'Fuck.' Tightens his grip on the grass in his fist. 'Now I *will* lose my job.'

A whole scenario fast-forwards through my head: poor gay boy tossed to the street, jobless, forced to sell his ass. It has its appeals. But no. I've seen too many take that trajectory: it never ends well, and I'm sure I shan't be responsible. I hoist myself vertical. 'Well, we don't want that, do we now?'

'Once the complaint gets filed, there'll be an investigation and…'

'And if the complaint gets withdrawn?' My mother always said, *I forgive but I never forget.* An oxymoron, if ever there was one. I have made it my life's mission to do everything in the opposite way to how she would have had it done. *Thou shalt take apprenticeship!* Ta very much, but I shall take the scholarship. *Thou shalt take a wife!* Yeah, thanks Mum, but I shall take it up the bum. The list goes on. 'I mean, I don't suppose Madam wants the Social sniffing round her drawers any more than I do. So perhaps we could make a deal…'

'Yeah—we tried that before, remember?' He looks at me, accusingly. 'Someone didn't stick to terms.'

'Let's say lessons have been learnt.' I look back, meaningfully. 'On both sides, I hope.'

He nods, almost imperceptibly.

I smile, almost discretely. 'Okay, well it's good stuff that— be a shame to waste it. Perhaps we might keep nicotine *and* cannabis under key and lock in that kitchen cabinet…?'

He shakes his head. 'She'd never agree…'

I offer my hand. 'She'd never need know about it, would she?'

He hesitates, seems about to accept; I pull my hand back.

'Let's sleep on it.'

He pulls his face up.

'Though heaven knows how I shall sleep without my marijuana nightcap.'

'Have you tried counting sheep?'

'I prefer chickens.'

And then he can't help smiling. 'What about wanking? Works for me every time.' He makes the gesture as he closes the door.

Cheeky bugger.

There was a time when I could wank for the European Union. Long gone. It all got somewhat… anticlimactic. And as for sexual *relations*—back in the day, I kept a tally. But now, really, who would want this old body? Everything went south at the end of the last century. I don't think there's been anyone since that gentleman in *The Champion* up at Notting Hill Gate, and that went straight in two thousand and… well, the years blur into one. He was no chicken, but he wanted to call me *Daddy* and everything; he wasn't so *very* bad-looking, so I let him. *Rien de rien* in the downstairs department. Never bothered again.

That fly is no longer bothering the windowpane—perhaps *Little Miss Muffet* brought a spider in with her. I'm just enjoying the peace and quiet when there is another knock at the door.

'Now what?'

'It's Jim.' His voice sounds alarmingly upbeat: even the door's fibreglass cannot mute it.

'And what do you want?'

'Can I come in?'

Oh gawd. I get the door.

He's stood there in the corridor like some antiquated suitor, in his hand a yellow flower. 'Catch.' He tosses it in the air.

I try not to guffaw and retrieve it from the floor. 'It's meant to be a bunch of them.' I refer, of course, to the Genet film. But see the reference is lost on him. 'And you swing them on a rope from your window to mine.' He still has no idea what I'm on about, poor thing; I usher him in and put wood in the hole behind him.

'So what happened?' He has a hand to his head; I realise he means my bandage.

'The story is long.' I begin to denude the rose of its thorns. 'What happened to your hand?'

'I tried to break free.'

'Really?'

'Didn't work, obviously.'

I make like some silent movie heroine, tied in a dungeon with a ravishing villain, and indulge in some silly flirting. 'You cannot mean, sir, that we are trapped here together?' Then, to complete the look, tuck the flower behind my unbandaged ear. 'Ta-dah!'

He smiles, porcelain and everything. 'You look lovely.'

'Please!' Praise is something I've always craved desperately and accepted uneasily. 'Spare me...'

He looks at me, seriously. 'Is that why you do it?'

'Do what?'

'The lipstick? The flamboyant clothing? Constantly putting

yourself in the firing line?'

'Here we go…' Why do people *always* want to fix you?

'Do you know, for years I couldn't even look at myself in a mirror.' Glass-eyed, he stares. 'Who is that person? And why are they still here?'

This is the most, and the most openly, he's ever spoken; I cannot countenance what might have wrought this change in him.

'We had one of those mirrored cabinets. Dickie bought it. He bought everything like that. One day I just opened it, swallowed its contents and waited…'

'Is that…?'

'That's why I'm in this place. With Dickie gone, I had no reason to go on.'

I had thought Dickie *gone* some time, but do not question his timeline: his *onset* obviously began somewhat *earlier* than mine; it would not be kind. And I would like to be kind. 'You know, I started an inferno.' I take his good hand in my own.

'How very unlike you.'

Oh no. Oh no, no, no. That look again.

He raises my hand to his lips. And kisses it.

I've never been attracted to guys my age. When I was younger, I liked them older. I liked a *man who was a man*. I know. Eyeroll. And then, one time—when I was still in my thirties—I went with this guy who was maybe in his fifties. Nice apartment. View of the Thames. Expensive wine. Everything. On his walls there were pictures of when he was young and handsome. I mean, he was still decent-looking. Chin not too gone. But when we undressed—his skin had a looseness, a smell to it. Like I was inhaling the dead cells he had shed. I never went back for seconds. And it was around then I leap-frogged to younger men. *Boys*. By which I mean, in their twenties.

'I'm really not your type.' I remove my hand from Jim's.

He looks like I removed an organ. 'What do you mean?'

'I, my dear, am an effeminate queer. Whereas you... are a respectable homosexual.'

I can see my nit-picking is lost on him. 'And?'

'Couldn't we just be friends?'

And I hug him, and then...

Well, I'm not entirely certain how it happens—perhaps he slips Rohypnol in my Complan—but we end up on the bed, still in all our clothing. And we stay in all our clothing. Cuddling, just cuddling. Not canoodling even. Purely and simply cuddling.

All throughout my forty days and nights in the desert, cock was not my biggest temptation. Yes, I missed it. And there were times I almost capitulated, ran into the streets, screaming—*call me Daddy, call me anything, just stick the damn thing in!* But if I'm honest, what I missed most were the hugs.

And now I am a cat rediscovering the pleasure of having her master's hand stroke her. And every time his hand stops stroking, I headbutt him for more. And deep within the cavity of me, I begin to purr—so loud I swear they can hear downstairs. And then, I suppose, my purr becomes a snore.

Because when I wake, it's dark. But somewhere there is light. Jim's belly is against my back—expanding and contracting— his hand is on *my* belly, resting. We are spooning; he is sleeping, his breath on my neck as I crane to find where the light is coming from.

The door is open and Craig is tiptoeing in like some pantomime villain, entrance music all hi-hats.

'It's not what you think.' I stage whisper to him.

He stops; I get a silhouetted crotch-shot as he takes his earphones out.

'I mean, look at him—he's an old man.'

'So are you, Joan.'

And I try for something droll about being as old as *who* you feel, but it doesn't come. 'So I am.'

He places two 'nightcaps' on the cabinet. 'Those are yours, and these are Jim's.'

'You know, I used to believe—when I was young—that one day I would find the perfect man.' And perhaps that's why they only ever lasted a few fucks, weeks, months—they were never quite completely right. And I could never be faffed to fix them.

'One man can never be everything you want.' The admittance of doubt, and perhaps deviation—these too are new developments.

'And is your husband in agreement on this?'

Craig shakes his head.

'So you're going behind his back?'

'I…'

'And you've just not been caught, yet.' I snort, the motion of my abdomen disturbing Jim; I freeze until he settles again.

Craig is smiling. 'I just assumed he was straight.'

'Get off the apps and open your eyes up.'

'Alright, Gramma. Maybe I'll try that.'

Little shit.

'You do remind me of my Gramma. She was quite a character.'

Always the *character*, never leading-lady.

'And tough—she had to be. She and Grampa came here in the fifties and, well, it wasn't easy. And then, in their seventies, they went back to St Lucia.' His eyes glisten in the light from the door. 'We never got to go see them out there.'

91

'So now we know why you care.'

'Sorry?'

'For us old codgers.'

He shrugs. 'Well, it was either that or gangster—according to the school careers officer.'

My own options had been hairdresser, or hooker.

'But soon as I'm a superstar DJ, I'll be out of here.'

He's about to spin off out the door again when I reach out to stop him.

He takes my hand. No words are exchanged. But we both understand.

It takes these old peepers of mine some moments to adjust to the darkness he leaves behind. A little light slips in through the open curtain—maybe it's even a moonbeam—illuminating Young Joan, up in his frame and looking down on this extraordinary scene.

I turn from him. And clasp my hand around Jim's, his sagging skin soft-scooped in mine.

Jim

He is sat in his usual chair. But nothing is usual anymore. He is not studying, not scouring a job section. He is not living in the past or the future. He is present; he is here. The same sun has climbed the same walls of the same sitting room, but the dust in its beam has rejigged its routines. Because Joan is sat beside him.

It is a Monday, and Mondays mean pampering. Manicure, pedicure and—every so often—hairdresser. Jim has been short-back-and-sided and is feeling like a pencil freshly sharpened. Joan has gone what he calls 'Full Quentin': his hair has a lavender shimmer in the sunshine.

Harold, sat one o'clock in their circle, has had his standard-issue: silver curls congregate at the sides of his pate as he puzzles over the Standard crossword. 'Fifteen down. To oil. Nine.'

The word pops into Jim's head and is as soon said. 'Lubricate!'

Craig stops painting Eileen's nails and starts giggling.

'Nine.' Jim can feel himself blushing.

Joan smiles in that impish way Jim is starting to enjoy. 'Of course.' He squeezes Jim's hand. 'Clever man.'

For Jim, such public display of affection is a new thing. He and Dickie would never have held a hand. Or only in the cinema sometimes, with everyone's attention on the screen. Jim's instinct is to withdraw his fingers. But Joan's keep up their pressure.

Harold sucks his teeth, says nothing. Eileen is staring, but also stays silent. Her hair has been blow-dried into a bouffant reminiscent of Thatcher in her decline. There is a redness around her eyes to match her nail polish. And a sadness Jim has never noticed before. *Poor dear.* She really was barking up the wrong tree. But then she didn't know—*how could she?* He wonders whether she and Harold might not get it together. Of late, they've seemed thick as thieves with each other. But then, as Joan has whispered in Jim's ear with not a little laughter, Harold does seem to have eyes only for young 'Princess' Eugenia; Joan has taught Jim the association game: it really does work wonders on names.

The chair beside Eileen is empty. Anya—as in *ain't ya*, as in *quiet*, except when she's wailing—is in the dining room having her hair 'done'. Last time this happened she returned without her usual bun, ringleted like *Baby Jane*.

Was that Joan Crawford? *No, it was the other one.*

The final chair is due to be filled again. 'Everyone!' And right on cue, Ms Mirza appears, claps her hands. 'I would like to introduce our new resident.'

Joan turns to Jim. 'Didn't take long to clear Mary's room.'

'They never do.' It is Jim's turn to squeeze Joan's hand.

Harold looks up from counting letters on *his* hands, and Eileen's neck cranes as a woman wheels herself in with dour-faced determination.

'This is Maude.' She has short, mannish hair. She wears shirt and trousers.

Nothing is usual anymore.

It is not until later, upstairs, that there is opportunity to discuss this matter. 'So, the new one—what do you reckon?' Joan is at Jim's shoulder

'She seems perfectly pleasant. If somewhat stern.' Jim is opening his door. This evening, he has not waited to see if Joan will invite him in: he has invited Joan.

'I think she's a *filthy* lesbian.'

'I think you may be leaping to conclusions.'

Even though the fixtures and fittings are not Jim's own—indeed, are things he could never conceive of owning—it feels like flashing.

'The lesbians were always good at leaping into action—like when they leapt into the Lords that time. You could rely on a lesbian to get the job done.'

'Do sit down.' Jim settles on the bed and allows Joan to take the chair.

Joan perches on the edge of it, as if uncertain if he should be there. 'It's very... minimalist. Don't you miss your home comforts?'

'Home is where the heart is.'

'Load of old rubbish.'

'Is it?' The semi-detached Jim had shared with Dickie had, on his death, become a house, merely.

'Is this...?' Joan is squinting at the image on the bedside cabinet.

'Dickie, yes.' Jim had never got used to the emptiness on Dickie's side of the mattress. He would reach out in his sleep, wake empty-handed and, in that second between sleeping and waking, lose him all over again.

'Would you mind?' Joan is already reaching for the photograph.

Fearing the smart of one of his remarks, Jim plays defensive. 'You might think him not much to look at, but...'

'You loved him.'

'I did.' From almost the moment he had seen him across that conference floor—sandy-haired, rosy-lipped. And when he'd opened those lips and Jim had heard that Scottish accent...

A knock. Joan props the photo back up, and replies with his signature call-back. 'Oh yes?'

95

The door cracks open; they hear a voice teasing, 'Are you both decent?'

'One second!' Joan beckons Jim towards him. Jim hesitates, uncertain of Joan's intentions. Joan grabs hold of Jim's hand. Jim groans upright again. Joan puts his hands about Jim's buttocks and levels his head with the belt of Jim's trousers. Jim stiffens, in more places than one: he's not been in such a compromising position in more years than he might care to mention.

'Come in!' Joan sets his head bobbing.

Jim isn't sure if he does or doesn't want Joan to see what's happening in the trouser department. And with the door now behind him, Jim can only imagine what the young care-assistant must be making of the scene he's walked in on.

'Argh!' Craig shrieks at a pitch which seems to indicate he understands it's a set-up. 'Gross!'

Joan releases his hands from Jim's hips and plants them on his own. 'Because we're not twenty-something, muscle-bound, and wearing fake orange tan?'

Jim turns to see Craig's eyes rolling. 'Stick that in it.' He thrusts a pill cup at Joan. 'I see you finally unpacked then?' He proffers another to Jim. 'This one must be having *some* positive influence.'

Who would have thought it, such a short time back? But, *yes*. 'He is.'

'Cheers!'

'Cheers!'

They clink 'glasses'. Down the hatches. Jim wonders what's in Joan's 'cocktail', as he calls it. They've not had that conversation, yet.

'Who is this?' Craig has spotted the photo on the cabinet; he seems in talkative mood tonight.

Jim hesitates, of habit. 'My partner.' It feels good to give voice to it, for Craig to hear it; Jim notes he's not wearing his ear-things this evening.

'Ah!' Craig picks the photo up, doesn't ask permission. 'And how long were you together, if you don't mind me asking?'

'Well, it would have been thirty years…'

'Thirty!'

'Had he not died a few months before.' Jim returns buttocks to bed; this is a conversation that requires him to be sitting down. There had been ups and downs with Dickie, certainly, in the course of their three decades: that time when Jim's suspicions had been confirmed about those strolls in Kensington Gardens of an evening. But generally, they'd been happy.

'I'm sorry.' Craig restores the photograph to its rightful place.

Jim knows he has a partner, but has never even considered asking about him before. 'How long have you and your...?'

'Husband.'

How strange it still seems to hear. 'How long have you been together?'

'Three years in December, if we make it that far.'

Joan pulls a face like he's inhaling icy air. 'Oh dear.'

Jim offers something warmer to reassure. 'Takes a lot of give and take to stay together.' Eventually, they'd stopped trying to make each other 'better', accepted one another the way that they were. 'You'll get there.'

'Yeah.' Craig doesn't seem confident, changes the subject. 'So, by way of thanks for withdrawing your complaint…'

Jim has no idea what he's talking about. 'Our what?'

Joan holds his hands up. 'Nothing you need worry your pretty head about.'

Jim, no fan of secrets, thinks, *we'll see about that.*

97

'I got you a present.' Craig pulls something from his pocket. 'Catch.'

Neither Jim's nor Joan's reactions are quick enough, and whatever-it-is falls to the floor at their feet. Joan is first to get the joke. And get to the packet. 'Well, I do hope they're ribbed for extra sensation.'

The room rings with Craig's laughter. 'I think there's also some lubricant in there.'

This raises a laugh from Joan. But for Jim, the gift raises a spectre. Safer sex is also not a conversation they have had yet. It took some decades for Jim and Dickie to have it. When they'd met, the disease was just a nasty rumour. And later… well, why would they need bother when they only made love to each other? Then Jim had found out about the other men. And that had been devastating, but also frightening. Dickie gave apologies, assurances—he'd been safe with each and every one of them. Nevertheless, Jim had taken himself for a test; the result took a white-knuckle week to come back. It was negative; the negative effects on their relationship took longer than seven days to repair: trust had to be rebuilt from the very first square.

'But seriously…' Craig is doing that thing they do, where they squat down *to your level*. The material of his uniform does not leave much to the imagination as his legs spread open; Jim isn't sure where he may safely put his eyes.

'Oh, please…' Joan's eyes are rolling at this turn in the conversation.

'Madam has been dissuaded—by yours truly—from having you extradited by social services.'

'Me?' Joan puts a hand to his chest as if receiving a wound there.

Jim feels like he missed an episode in a long-running drama.

Craig shakes his head. 'Not least because...' He is choosing his words. 'Well, it appears to us that the two of you may be embarking on some sort of relationship.'

A *relationship*? Goodness. Is that already what they're calling it? A cuddle. A hand held. But not yet a kiss. Not fully on the lips. And as for the rest... Well, certainly there had been no sex.

'Yes...' On Joan's face there is an expression like a challenge.

It isn't apparent if that challenge is meant for himself or for Jim. But in the downstairs department, Jim feels himself rising again; he hears himself repeating, 'Yes.'

'So we thought we'd give you a little more time in the hope you might... settle in.'

'Thank you.' Jim is quite genuine.

'Thanks.' Joan's tone is somewhat disparaging.

Craig stands, winks in Jim's direction. 'Can't believe I tried to fix you up with Eileen.'

'Eileen!' Joan escalates to derision.

Jim searches for a platinum lining. 'Maybe she might get it together with... the new one.'

'You mean Maude?' Craig frowns.

'Yes, Maude.' *As in...*

Joan gets there first. 'Harold and!'

And they all laugh again. Then Joan starts coughing. Through thin chiffon, Jim can see Joan's thin frame contorting. 'Are you okay?'

'It's nothing.' The dislodgement of phlegm seems as dramatic as an exorcism.

Craig spirits a tissue from a pocket, gives it to Joan— and a look to Jim. 'Well you know where I am if you need anything.' He sets his hand at a steep angle of elevation. 'Like a prescription.'

Cheeky thing.

When he closes the door behind him, Craig leaves a suggestion in the room—a shoot surfacing, not yet spoken. Unable to give voice to it, Jim changes the subject. 'What's this complaint he was on about?'

Joan tucks the tissue away. 'Oh, it was nothing, really.'

'Somehow, you don't convince me...'

'Well, let's just say he was a very bad boy and I had to smack his little bottie.'

'Which you did, only reluctantly.'

'And which he enjoyed...' Joan scans his dictionary. 'Inordinately.'

Jim scans his memory. 'I can't believe I had him down as...'

'Straight-acting only, that one.'

'I suppose I just assume that...' Jim wants to find the best way of putting it, without sounding foolish. Or plain prejudiced. 'That black men... Are all like...' *Mary—Wilson.* 'Harold.' Next time, he'll get it in one.

'Ignorance is the mother of assumption.'

This sounds like a conclusion, but leaves Jim with more questions. 'Have you...?'

'A fair few.'

'And do...?'

'Not all clichés are true.'

And with the thought of dark skin, there it is again: like dark soil, freshly turned—in spring, in the garden—that earthy smell arising; the sense of something about to happen. Jim squints down at his watch-hands; the night is still a handsome young man. 'So...' He knows it's never or now.

'Best get to bed then.' Joan is still side-stepping.
But now, Jim is leading. 'Yours or mine?'

Joan

'And then he took out his dentures!'

'No!'

'Yes. Popped them on the bedside cabinet and got down to business.'

We're both roaring. And in the sitting room, necks are craning. The cat is among the pigeons: Gladys has come visiting, wearing best marbled denim.

'And how was it?'

'Toothless!'

Again, we roar. *Oh, how I've missed her.* I'd wanted to give the 'tour'. Around the 'gardens'. Out there, no one's listening. But when she saw it spitting, she refused to step from the door lest the rain make a disaster of what remains of her *riah*. So we're sat in the dining room sipping tepid tea from cheap china, Eileen's clucks and Harold's tooth-sucks reaching our ears from around the corner; recently they have taken to expressing their disapproval solely via non-verbal means. Anya is away with the fairies, as ever, and Maude, I'm sure, has heard it all before.

I drop to stage whisper. 'But seriously, nothing.' I sign to my groin. 'It was like a little acorn.'

Gladys waves a manicured hand. 'I get all my erections online.' She loves a blue diamond. 'And don't even think of asking.' Now a finger is wagging. 'I'm not your drug mule, darling.'

It's true, she has—at my behest—already fetched in something *grass green* to supplement DJ Craigie's rations. Though she stopped short of smuggling the baggy in her saggy old bottom.

'I'm just not sure I fancy him.'

'Well, you've never had much taste in men. Remember that punk with the piercings?'

'Please don't!'

'You were all over him. Until you got your perm caught in his Prince Albert. And then there was the one that…'

Our volume has risen again. Princess Eugenia emerges around the partition, hands primly clasped atop plastic apron. 'Everything alright?'

Gladys is all snow-white smile. 'Everything's perfect.'

'You want more tea?'

'No.' I am cold as the pot on the table. 'We'd just like some privacy.'

The princess nods in that passive aggressive way of hers. I make a face as she withdraws.

'You know Joan, it doesn't *have* to be a battle.' Gladys purses cat's arse lips.

'Oh, but it always is.'

'Maybe she was just trying to be helpful?'

I remain unconvinced.

Gladys decants dregs from the teapot into her cup, adds milk and sugar to it. 'So how was it for *him*?' She starts stirring. 'Don *Jim* of the Care Home.'

He'd been patient, understanding. 'Well, there wasn't any problem with his engineering.'

'For an octogenarian, that is quite something.'

He'd been vanilla as an ice-cream. 'But when I tried to put a finger up him, he nearly hit the ceiling.'

Gladys' jaw hits the vinyl table-covering.

'And he's all *I'm a top! I'm a top!* and I'm *right, pass me the lubricant, we'll see about that…*'

And then, I see him—in the sitting room, hesitating.

Oh, buggeration.

I shoot a sharp look to stop Gladys squawking, smile as if there's nothing to be seen, and—hoping he's not heard anything—beckon Jim in.

He's looking dapper as ever this afternoon, tie and pocket handkerchief matching. *Blue on the left—what does that mean?* He stops just inside the partition, not quite completely in the dining room. He offers Gladys an outstretched thumb and four fingers. 'Hello there.'

Gladys doesn't demur. 'Charmed, I'm sure.'

'Jim, Gladys. Gladys, Jim.' I feel like a teenager taking home his first boyfriend.

Old Glad-eyes twinkles. 'I've heard so much about you.'

Jim raises a brow. 'Have you?'

'All of it flattering.'

'Somehow, I doubt that.' His intonation seems to confirm he's overheard something. And that I shall probably be in the hound-house later on.

But for now, I glide away, execute a *fouetté*. 'How was your lesson?'

'Confusing.' Craig has been showing him how to get online.

'Darling, at our great age, most things are.'

Gladys snickers. 'Like that time when I found you roaming corridors in your knickers?'

'I couldn't find the right door!'

'My dear, you were on the wrong floor.'

I try not to slip as I finish my pirouette. 'Well there were about seven of them.'

'You were only looking for the bathroom.'

Bitch. Even Jim's face cracks a bit.

'Won't you join us?' Gladys invites him to take a seat at our table.

'No, I shan't disturb you. Just popped in to say *hello*.'

'You're not disturbing us at all. Is he, Joan?'

'No.' My inflection does not convince Jim, obviously.

'I'm sorry. All that technology has quite exhausted me.'

'Poor dear. I'll be up a bit later.'

'Oh, don't worry. You enjoy each other's company. I expect I shall turn in early.'

I'm surprised at my disappointment. 'Alright.' Obviously, I'll be sleeping in my own room tonight. But at least I can have a narcotic nightcap to help me off, with Gladys' supplies now in my pocket.

As I watch Jim shuffle off with a *lovely to meet you*, I am surprised at my sadness to see him go. As I turn back to Gladys, I do not let this show.

'Well…' Her eyebrows Jean Harlow. 'I shall now be able to file my report in full.'

Gladys is listed as 'next of' in the abstinence of 'kin' and has, hilariously, received a tip-off from Madam about my 'relationship' with Jim.

'But, *entre nous*, I approve.'

'Really?' It would seem I shall not be receiving the critique I've been expecting, coveting even.

'He's a sweetheart, that one.' Her glad-eyes now glisten. 'And if you don't want him, I'll have him.' She's been foraging for a father figure ever since her own daddy showed her the door: the fact that she's getting moist about getting it together with some over-courteous old codger—I mean really—it says less about me and more about *her*.

I shrug my shoulders. 'He's just such a square.'

'Take what you can, darling. Won't get the chance again.'

Her eyes scythe to the corners of the room—as if seeking cobwebs, or death—before settling again on mine. 'I think you know what I'm saying.'

Indeed, I know exactly what she's saying. And quite unprepared for this mortal confrontation, find myself floundering. 'It's… It's… It's just not happening!'

'It's not about sex!' This from Gladys.

In the living room, Eileen tuts again; with that woman the only other option, it's no wonder it's with me that Jim threw his lot in. 'It's not even about romance!' Gladys goes on.

Well, I would have loved nothing better than for Cupid to take wing, for the strings to start soaring, but both have been staying stubbornly earthbound.

'It's about companionship!' Gladys lays her trump card with a flourish.

I can't help guffawing. 'Have you been reading *The Lady* again?'

The glad-eyes glare. 'I've seen it before. That Spaniard…'

'Victor?'

'He was a keeper.'

'Knob like a bent banana.' I try to steer conversation onto less serious ground. 'So they're not all straight in the European Union.'

But Gladys looks like she sucked-off a lemon, 'No one is ever perfect. Even you, Joan.'

An extraordinary assertion. And I am seeking something extraordinary to say in return, when she takes my hand.

'You know, I have always admired you, John.'

Uh-oh. The name-peel.

'And I have always admired your passion.'

Gladys and I met through shared passion. Politics and men. She was one of a rolling cast of young queens—full of spunk and slogans—at those early Liberation Front meetings. Older, colder, I rolled up to the first one hoping it might be full of hot totty. But it was the politics that were eye-opening for me.

'You were the one on every demonstration.' With her free hand, she pats *Bride of Frankenstein* hair down. 'Whether or not it was raining.'

It's true, I can weather a storm—thrive, even, on tribulation. And it's true that, as Saint Saul after conversion, activism became my obsession: nothing was more important than liberation. Even the boyfriends took a backseat to my crusade for complete freedom.

'Your activist days are over.' She lowers her hand to join the other, my own hand smothered. 'But you can still be a passionate *lover*.'

I wrest it back from her. 'Ha!' To me, passion poured into one man is passion of a peevish kind when compared to the passion for *all* mankind.

Gladys checks no nails are broken. 'Now tell me what you *do* like about him.'

Well... My gob goes goldfish. *He is well-travelled, well-educated.* I do not say this. *I tell him about the opera houses I've worked in; he tells me all about the way they built them.* To say this would be admission. *And when you start to break it down, the engineering of a building and that of a frock are not so very different.* Admission that there could be something in common, something for which it might be worth persevering.

'Just *one* thing, Joan.'

'The flowers,' I admit.

Gladys shakes her head.

'I thought I told you about them?'

Gladys sets her head at a resigned incline.

'So, every day since I was attacked mercilessly with a mobility aid, he fetched me a flower from the garden…' After that first rose, a sweet pea—the same routine, behind his back and me all, *really?* But then, the scent of that one bloom filling my room, filling my head with silly notions. And the next day, a peony. A hydrangea, the day after. 'Until management had a word with him. Said the flowers are for everyone.'

I can see Gladys is getting moist again. 'That is *so* lovely.'

I've always avoided the easy, the cliché.

'You are *so* lucky.'

What was it they said on that retreat—back when I thought it would turn out right overnight if I lit a few joss sticks and stopped eating meat—something about avoidance of habit *becoming* the habit?

'Most girls would kill for that.'

I swat away sentiment, reflexively. 'Honestly, you sound like my Mum.'

'She sounds like a sensible woman.'

She was a *sensitive* woman, who couldn't bear the thought of having a sensitive son. 'She was a gorgon.'

'So that's where you get it from.'

When I was younger, I couldn't bear the idea of being anything like my mother. But as I got older—and applied my mascara—it was her eyes that looked back from the mirror, stony as sapphire. 'I turn them all rock hard, you mean?'

'But are *you* made of stone, Joan?'

We roar once more, without caring who's listening. And if I keep roaring, I can't hear that voice, questioning.

What might it mean to once more be molten?

Jim

As the doors open, he sees her. Hair grey, groomed. Clothing polished, professional. She is sat at the table in the dining room, poring over something—a phone—thumb tapping, as though determined not to waste a moment of time as she waits for colleagues to join.

Or perhaps she is waiting for just one person. For Jim. Perhaps this is interview, not meeting. An opportunity for which, until recently, he has been longing. But now he finds himself feeling unprepared for any questions she might ask him and is turning back to the elevator's mirrored interior to check his tie is at least straightened, when its doors tell him they are closing…

'Uncle Jim!'

The illusion is broken; the woman is rising, rushing towards him to hold the doors open.

'How wonderful to see you again!'

Then she is embracing him, enveloping him in something expensive smelling. And it's overwhelming: his first fight with Joan, the knock at the door—not to tell them to quieten down but to tell Jim he had a visitor…

Receiving no reciprocation, she pulls back, seeks recognition. 'It's this, isn't it?' She pats at her hair. 'Does it make me look older?'

He has no idea to what earlier incarnation he is meant to compare her: he is quite sure he's never met her before.

'The colour's been growing out for… Can it really have been two years?'

Why is she there? And why she is being so familiar?

'It's me, Melissa.'

Melissa?

'Catherine's daughter.'

Catherine. His sister.

'Honestly, I feel dreadful that I've not been to see you before. Of course, we are hardly ever here these days—you know we bought in Mousehole, after Mummy passed away?'

The crematorium. She was still brunette back then.

'And when we are in town, there never seems time to fit everything in. I've been meaning to come but... Well, life always seems to throw something up.'

The hospital. Whispering with the doctor.

'Oh, how thoughtless of me!' Today, her voice is full velocity. 'You must want to sit down.'

It's true, Jim can feel ground shifting; she steers him into the dining room.

'Oh Uncle, I have so much to tell you! Can you believe Christopher is getting married!'

The garden. A boy. In fact, two of them. Trampling Dickie's dahlias down.

'Such a shame you can't come to the wedding.'

Jim is not aware of having received invitation.

'I know Chris would've loved to have you there.' She parks Jim in a chair. 'He still speaks so fondly of his Great Uncle Jim. *And* his Great Uncle Dickie. So, tell me...' She perches on the chair beside him. 'How are *you* doing?'

'You are doing well, are you not, Jim?' And then, Ms Mirza is speaking for him. 'He is starting to settle in.' She has appeared from somewhere and is addressing this niece, who has appeared from nowhere, as if Jim isn't there. 'He has even made a *friend*.'

'A friend! How fantastic!' The niece speaks over Jim's head; he feels like it is parents' evening again, and there is some code passing between them he is not meant comprehend.

'Now, can I get you both tea?' Boss Lady has never previously staffed the canteen; something is afoot, of this, Jim is certain.

'Tea would be lovely! Milk, no sugar, please.'

'Two teas coming up!' And without awaiting response from Jim, she is gone again.

'She seems a nice lady.' Jim's niece looks at him then, for agreement.

He doesn't offer any, still completing his survey of the way this new land lies.

'In fact, they all seem nice here.'

Jim doesn't concur, begins to get a measure: Gladys' visit, the tip-off—how Joan had laughed, then their tiff.

'So, tell me about your friend…' She places her words down, as if she has rehearsed them. 'What is *their* name?'

'Joan.' Now Jim has some understanding of the terrain, he can begin to answer her questions.

'Joan. That's a lovely name!' She will not be winning Oscars anytime soon. 'And how long have you known… *her*?'

'Him.'

'The pronouns can be *so* confusing.' She bites a lip which looks well-bitten. 'So Joan is a *man*?'

'Correct.'

'How unusual.'

'Is it?'

Her mouth opens; the lift 'pings' in synchronisation. Over the woman's shoulder, he sees Joan emerge from the elevator. Upstairs, a few minutes earlier, Jim had been confronting him over indiscretions overheard yesterday in this very room, and

111

Joan had been denying all allegations. It is not an argument he is looking forward to continuing, certainly not with an audience.

'And are you... *close* friends?'

Jim isn't sure of the answer: he's not sure closeness is even in Joan's repertoire. 'Why don't you ask him yourself?'

As lift doors close behind Joan, and Joan spots the two of them in the dining room, Jim can only resign himself to whatever may now happen.

Jim's niece follows his eyeline. Her reaction is perhaps not dissimilar to Jim's own, on first seeing Joan. But then she immediately slaps a smile on. 'Hello!'

By Joan's standards, today's outfit is understated: white trousers, black shirt with pink flamingos on it and a trace of matching lipstick. He is making a beeline towards them; there is sadly no one sitting in the sitting room to impede him.

'And you must be Joan!' Her tone is as patronising as a primary schoolmistress. Joan is now close enough for Jim to see plumage puff beneath flamingo fabric; he thinks, actually, he might enjoy this. And that—if the niece gets it—he may be spared at least.

'The very same.' Joan speaks with exaggerated decorum through an exaggerated grin, which gives him the air of an evil fairy in an old Walt Disney film. 'And whom do I have the pleasure of addressing?'

'Melissa.' She extends a hand. Joan takes it. Raises it to his lips. Jim follows her eyeline to the bangles at Joan's wrist. 'I'm Jim's niece.'

'I had no idea he had one.' Joan releases her hand, turns his attention to Jim. 'Closed book, this one.'

Jim thinks that rich, from Joan—whose cover may be generously gilded, but who rarely reveals the contents of his pages. Although at present, he does appear to be attempting to communicate something; Jim cannot read whatever message Joan's eyebrows may be morsing.

'Never a man of many words, Uncle Jim.' Her smile seems affectionate. 'I'm glad he's found a friend.'

'A friend?' Joan's eyes pivot in her direction. 'How *very* twentieth century.' He has somehow located a lock of Jim's hair through which to twirl a finger. 'My dear, your uncle and I are lovers.'

Jim sits, frozen, in his chair. *That's that question answered.*

His niece, however, continues to thaw; she unexpectedly guffaws. 'Well, I'm glad that's clear.' And then gestures to the seat across from her. 'There's tea coming—you'd be welcome to join.'

'Thank you kindly, but I am otherwise engaged this morning.'

'Oh, that is a shame.'

'I just…' His eyebrows are doing that thing again. 'Well, we weren't expecting a visit and I wanted to check that everything's alright.'

Joan's code finally becomes clear. *And Jim never knew he cared.*

'Everything's fine, isn't it, Uncle Jim?'

And perhaps everything is fine. Perhaps he has got it all mixed up again. About Joan. About this niece who has so suddenly found him. Jim finds himself nodding.

'I'll be in my room. Come up and see me sometime.' Joan cannot resist a parting salvo of innuendo as he heads for the elevator. 'Lovely to meet you, uh…'

'Melissa!'

'Charmed, I'm sure!' Joan disappears behind lift doors, leaving Jim bewildered and alone with his niece once more. He looks at her, looking after Joan: beneath that professional grooming, there is a pallidness to her skin and a restlessness to her hands, now she has nothing to occupy them.

'Well, Joan seems… *fun.*' She turns to him, smiling and frowning. 'Uncle Jim, I hope you won't mind me asking, but I thought you liked men?'

'Joan *is* a man.'

'You know what I mean. Uncle Dickie could camp it up a bit sometimes, but he was very much a man. Joan, on the other hand…'

'We're all on a spectrum.' Jim hears himself saying something oft-declaimed by Joan.

'Well, I'm not sure I am. But then…' Suddenly she spans the table with her hand. 'Uncle, I just want you to be happy.'

And then, he can't find anything to say.

'I mean, I'd hate to think Joan was only after you for your money.' Her inflection is jesting; her intention perhaps has bigger bells on.

An alarm is ringing for Jim—*there is something about this woman and his home and*—he withdraws his hand. 'Joan has no interest in money.'

'I didn't mean… I'm sorry.'

'And anyway, I don't have any!' Jim makes to stand: he finds her insinuation offensive and, given Joan's daily diatribes against private ownership, quite ridiculous and—*that's it, yes, this is the woman who sold his house off!*

'Well, that's just not true: the money is all in an account for you; we all want you to receive the best care possible. Uncle…' Again, she takes his hand—more firmly this time—so he has no choice but to stay sat down. 'I just want you to know that if you're not happy here, then… Well, we can look at other options. Rashida…' Her voice drops lower. '…says this affair has been rather sudden, and that shortly before it came to her attention, you had seemed intent on…'

114

'Tea's up!' Again, Ms Mirza is upon them—setting pot, cups, saucers, spoons, milk jug, sugar bowl, and even a plate of biscuits before them. Probably she is simply doing her job—protecting those under her protection. And as someone who always prided themselves in their work, Jim should find this a source of admiration. But he can't help wondering if she would be quite so zealous over the interests of her heterosexual residents. And he does detect some embarrassment in her expression as she is leaving. Though that may be due merely to his niece's over-enthusiasms.

'Well, this looks amazing! Shall I be Mum?' She makes a great show of pouring, adding milk afterwards. Dickie always said the milk should go in first. She offers Jim a biscuit; he demurs—digestives don't mix well with dentures. She dunks hers. Dickie thought that common. But then, quite probably, he would have thought Joan common. Dickie would not have understood the attraction. Jim is not certain he understands.

'Uncle…'

But then, quite possibly, he is a ridiculous old man with amorous delusions.

'That thing you said…'

Quite likely their relationship is just one of last resort. In a doldrum, *any port.*

'About us all being on a spectrum.'

Lost in thought, Jim has quite forgotten the woman, and the tea sat before him.

'Do you really think that's true?'

Like many of Joan's pronouncements, it has the ring of truth about it. And yet it may not stand to be unpicked: just because Joan *says* they are lovers, does not mean they are, in fact.

'Well, we are all individual—but that doesn't mean we're all just one thing.'

Although Joan may sound effeminate, his approach is often brutishly 'masculine'; Joan's admission of affection, not in word but action, may tell more truth than any declaration.

'Red. Green. Man. Woman. Between complements there are other colours… so why not other genders?'

Just weeks earlier, such a line of thinking would have seemed inconceivable to Jim. But lines, he is learning, may be redrawn. And the way his niece is looking at him reminds Jim of a younger woman—sat, open, in their kitchen, before her own lines had been inked in. 'Uncle, may I talk to you about something?'

Jim nods. *Old dogs*—who says?

'Well—Christopher, as I told you, is settling down. Jack, on the other hand…'

The other boy—running about the garden.

'It's all been rather unsettling. First, there was the attempt on his life and then…' She winces. 'I'm sorry, how insensitive of me…'

With a gesture, Jim reassures her—bridge, water— encourages her; he may never have been a man of many words, but has always been a good listener.

'He's recently told us he's transitioning.'

The other—retrieving the broken-stemmed after they'd been trampled by the brother.

'Jack is now Jacqueline.'

Then arranging and rearranging them in an old Gluggle Jug in the kitchen.

'It's so very hard to understand, as a parent. I mean, I always knew he was different. I just assumed he was gay. And of course, I had no problem with that. We grew up with it.'

Uncle Jim, look—the fish is singing flowers.

'I always loved coming to stay with you and Uncle Dickie.' She is smiling, sincerely. 'Such a treat after all that strictness from Mummy.'

How could he not have seen the resemblance to his sister, those same sharp features?

'All those stately homes you used to take us to. Daddy called you the stately homos.' Her eyes are rolling. 'I didn't mind. You always let us run around the gardens. And we *always* got ice-cream.' Then her eyes are glistening. 'I just can't help feeling we did something wrong.'

This time it's Jim who reaches out a hand. 'Is Jack... Jacqueline. Is *she* happy?'

One hand grips his, the other dabs the corners of her eyelids. 'I think... she finally is.'

'Then that's what's important, isn't it?'

His niece nods, faintly. 'You always were a kind man—don't let anyone take advantage of that, Uncle Jim.'

He shakes his head, firmly.

Later, as he ascends alone in the elevator, he sees someone centred in its mirrored interior. As he shuffles down the corridor, a song from his youth worms his ear. *Que sera, sera.* As a teenager, Jim had tried to convince himself he fancied Doris Day. Of course, it was Rock Hudson he was interested in, really. *Whatever will be, will be.*

Arriving outside Joan's room, he hears another kind of music emerging from its interior. *Opera, always opera.* Jim has always been a jazz man, admiring its measured form. And its freedom. To transcend its structure, a standard requires the spontaneity of individual players—just as a formal garden requires the abundant anarchy of nature, and a classical colonnade the organic veining of each marble pillar. Jim can be too rigid, on his own; Dickie always understood the need for improvisation—in the kitchen, in the bedroom.

'It's open!' Joan is sat on his bed, listening. 'Got rid of her, then?'

'It all got rather emotional, in the end.'

Joan makes to stand. 'Let me turn this down.'

'It's fine.' Delaying the moment when he must start speaking, Jim sits beside Joan and listens. Something plucked. Something bowed. Above them, two vocals. Entwined in exquisite and excruciating harmony. In dissonance, beauty.

'Monteverdi.' Joan translates, as usual. 'I gaze upon you. I embrace you. I enchain you.'

'Didn't know you were into S&M.' Jim had tried it once, at Dickie's behest. Tied him to the bedposts. Had him call him 'Sir' and everything. Neither of them could stop laughing. Jim soon untied him.

'I draw the line at permanent marks.'

'So that's what I'm not doing right.'

Joan laughs, looks down at his lap. 'Darling, you're not doing anything wrong: it's me who has the problem.' He looks back up. 'I'm sorry for what you overheard yesterday afternoon. I've never been known as the soul of discretion.'

'Well, I'm...' This is the first time Jim is aware of hearing Joan express contrition; he feels it would be churlish not to reciprocate in some form. 'Sorry for being oversensitive.'

'The thing is... It doesn't work.' Again Joan's eyes fall to his lap.

Goodness, is that it? There was Jim worrying whether Joan got any pleasure from the things they had done when the problem had simply been one of engineering.

'I'm sorry to hear that but...' Jim weighs his words carefully. 'If you wanted...' Adds each to the scales only slowly. 'There are measures we might take…'

'I know that.' Joan is still looking at his lap. This is the first time Jim is aware of seeing him experience shame. We all lose something with which we find it difficult to make reconciliation. Jim is losing his mind, if not his erection.

'Or perhaps…' Jim has always loved this moment, the one when you know the deal is struck. 'You might prefer it…' But they've not committed to signing yet, and so you withdraw the contract. 'If we were to just leave it.'

Joan looks up. 'Is that what you want?'

'Perhaps we could be better *friends* than *lovers*.'

Joan does not assent or decline. 'You know, you're a good man and really not bad looking.'

This is where the 'but' comes. Jim fears he's got his calculations wrong.

'You're also a terrible old stick, with terrible halitosis.'

Jim releases his bated breath. 'Is it so bad?'

'Yes.' Joan reaches for the fingers Jim has raised to his lips. 'But there are measures we might take.' Joan presses those fingers between his. 'And, as you know, I *never* accept defeat.'

It is the first time Jim is aware of Joan initiating a kiss. He is self-conscious, reluctant to reciprocate; Joan's tongue shucks him open. Joan's breath tastes of lipstick, cigarettes, of bitterness, of regret. Sour bass notes. A sweet heart, which is surprising. And head as saline as an ocean.

Joan

Dearest, darling Gladys,

Greetings from deepest, darkest Devon. What an adventure this care home 'excursion' has been! Double-dipping in the sea, the rest of them shilly-shallying in the shallow end but—you know me, in for a penny—and Jim diving right in after me. We both agreed—once you ARE in, the water isn't so bad really. Then, at the fairground, Jim won a stuffed unicorn! Gave it to me with some other good stuffings. And the rock here has been hard as diamond—this part of the country has seen some quite uncharacteristic volcanic activity. The double mattress may also have had a role to play. Hotel nothing to write home about but from our window we have a corner of sunset, pink as candyfloss.

Almost fingering the bottom—I shall tell you ALL when I return.

x Joan

ps. this postcard is the sauciest I could lay hands on—hope you enjoy the beach-bums.

Jim

They are on a beach again; swallows swarm the skies above them. The sun is low, golden; a breeze is cool upon his skin. Summer is ending; autumn is coming. The care home heating is not yet on.

With the coolness comes consciousness. He lies not on sand but on a mattress. A heat-seeking missile, he reaches and rolls. He is stiff and he is slow, but has not far to travel: the bed is a single. He's not shared a bed so small since his bones were young, in that Kensington bedsitting room, when such close confines had not seemed a problem—had been exciting, even. But two grown men, with two lifetimes' accumulations of pain— well, there are nights when they've just given up. When one or other of them has slunk back to their own room in the early hours of morning. And probably this is what has happened: Joan has returned next door for some quality shut-eye; Jim's arms return empty.

He opens his own eyes. The first thing floating into focus is Dickie's photograph. Jim wonders—probably not for the first time—if Dickie has minded sitting there watching them. But—who is Jim kidding—he's probably loving every moment. *Kinky bugger.* Jim presses his lips together, recalling the time that Dickie had wanted to bring a boy back, and Jim wasn't having any of it. That sort of thing wasn't for Jim. Still wouldn't be, really. He suspects Dickie had the boy back anyway.

On the occasions he's woken in Joan's room, the first thing swimming into Jim's field of vision has been the photo of Young Joan. He wonders—again, probably not for the first time— what their choices of picture say about them, but does not care to come to any conclusion.

Dickie's photo is now framed, flimsily. Viewed electronically, the frame had seemed perfectly sturdy. Craig had made picture-after-picture appear on a screen which usually sat sheathed downstairs in a side room. Beside him—a child in a sweetshop again—Jim had pointed and said *that one*. Somehow, Craig had purchased the oaken frame, and it arrived by post the following afternoon, to some disappointment. Its wood was all 'effect'—no wonder then, that it had been within Jim's price range.

Jim has always been independent, financially: he has never needed a handout from anybody. It had not been a pleasant realisation for him when Ms Mirza had sat him down and explained—or explained again—that, although he has does have money, it is no longer his to freely spend. And that, like Joan's cigarettes—which Jim so detested—it may only be metered in miniscule doses.

Joan may no longer be there, but his rings and things—removed before sleeping—still gather before Dickie's picture. Dickie's watch seems quite at home amongst them. Jim bought it for him and wears it in remembrance of him, though in truth, it is too tight on his wrist and not quite to his taste. Its gold blends seamlessly with Joan's... Well, one must not say *costume jewellery* because, of course, Joan does not wear a costume.

Joan's *clothing* often gets left about Jim's room. He tries not to let this get to him, though this is easier said than done: he's lived some time alone. How much time he couldn't say exactly, but long enough for the habit of forbearance to lie forgotten. He has, however, not forgotten how very bad he was at being on his own, and so loves to discover little reminders of his lover—a hair clip on the bedside cabinet, a hair in the bathroom sink. Joan had seemed self-conscious about his grey pubic hairs until

Jim had assured him they were, in fact, silver.

For someone so forthright about most things, Joan's diffidence around sex has been surprising to Jim. In the end, it was he who had gone to Craig for a prescription, asked for it written in his own name. And things had taken a bit of a turn then.

Hearing coughing, Jim realises he is not, in fact, alone. The cough passes quickly, thankfully—sometimes they seem to last an eternity. Jim has given up trying to convince Joan to quit smoking; as one gets older, the pleasures get smaller, and Jim had neither heart nor right to take this little pleasure from him. Though he is not to smoke on the balcony of Jim's room: on this Jim has been firm; the balcony is where he finds Joan standing, beatified by morning sun. The door is open behind him—explaining the breeze which had woken Jim.

Joan is most beautiful when he first wakes up. Without his make-up. Though Jim would never tell him that. And Joan would never believe he doesn't need it. That his eyes sparkle without any shadow. Jim cannot see them now, turned as they are toward the garden, its greens blurring into yellow and orange. Watching nature is another of Joan's pleasures. Jim takes a pleasure of his own in watching Joan.

His kimono-cum-dressing-gown is fluttering in the wind. If it were a costume, it is the kind of thing one might imagine... *what's her name?* Joan has continued apace with Jim's opera education, and this one is set in Japan... *Madame Butterfly!* It is the kind of thing one might imagine her wearing. It accentuates a broadness of shoulder. The slenderness of midriff. Jim worries sometimes that Joan is too thin. But just at this moment, with the sheen and the sunshine, his buttocks are a vision.

Sensing himself seen, Joan turns back into the room.

Jim cannot but smile at him. 'You're early.'

'Always am these days.' Joan smiles back at Jim.

'What's happening?'

'Whatstheirnames have been here again.'

'Jean and Genet?'

'Little vixens.'

Joan has a particular soft spot for the foxes of whom they catch fleeting glimpses. Jim doesn't much like the racket they make, but who is he to speak? One time, post-prescription, he and Joan raised such a racket that a complaint was raised by another resident. It amuses Jim to imagine Harold, in the next room along, crossing himself to the rhythm of their lovemaking.

Jim lets out another involuntary exclamation as he levers himself towards a sitting position.

'Is that back of yours playing up again?' Joan hurries over to help him.

'It's difficult, isn't it? The two of us in one little bed.'

Joan kisses Jim on his open-plan forehead. 'Would you have it any different?'

Not for the world, thinks Jim as he changes from nightwear to daywear. Trousers, shirt, blazer. *But a double-bed would make all the difference.* In this home, there are no other couples. No doubles, bed or room. He wonders—undoubtedly not for the first time—what it might take to procure one.

A knock at the door disturbs Jim's musings.

'Oh yes?' Joan has done dressing and is sat at a makeshift dressing table preparing to put make-up on.

The door opens just a crack. 'Breakfast.' Princess Eugenia has popped her head in. Which is quite something: when first she came across the two of them in one room, she all but ran down the corridor screaming.

'We'll be down soon.' Jim smiles in her direction; her head

nods and pops back behind the door, comedy fashion. 'Well, I wonder what today will bring?' He doubles-over and digs his heels in: laces are quite beyond him; he has had to embrace the slip-on.

'The possibilities are endless.' Joan is applying lipstick. 'We could... play cards?'

'You're a bad loser.'

'Watch Casablanca?'

'Again.'

'Perhaps we should take up knitting?'

'We don't have any offspring.'

'Did I not tell you?' Joan slaps his belly.

'Then we must get married.' It comes out accidentally, only half-playfully. But the proposal, Jim realises, is something he's been postulating for some time. Since their holiday to North Devon. Its landscape had reminded Jim of Scotland, and such synchronicity had not been lost on him—that last expedition with Dickie, his first with Joan. It had felt like something of a honeymoon, not least because they'd been able to share a double bed and room.

Joan is taken aback for but a moment. 'Only if I can wear the full meringue.'

'If it takes a frouffy white frock to make you an honest man, then fine.'

Joan doesn't return the serve this time, turns from the mirror to look at him. 'Are you serious?'

This is probably not the way he would have planned to pop the question, but Joan is teaching him to embrace things as they happen. 'I think I am.'

Joan's grin is condescending. 'That's terribly sweet of you, young man, but I am not the marrying kind.' And he returns to his reflection.

Jim doesn't know why he's disappointed: it is what he would have expected. 'I'm to take that as a *no*, I guess.'

'Why don't we do *your* lips?' Joan shifts subject.

Jim is having none of it. 'What is it you're afraid of?'

'*I* am not afraid of *anything*.' In a move more suited to the scale of La Scala, Joan's head pivots and his arms arc the air.

'Except perhaps acceptance?' Jim's breath would barely ruffle a feather.

But Joan seems to feel the weight of those words, landing. 'I'll take *that* as a no then.' He winds his neck and lipstick in.

Jim watches Joan—pretending not to be watching Jim, mirror-framed—then reaches for his own stick, the one he uses for walking. 'Well, the offer will stand. Now, let's see if I can.' He tries to lighten things up again as he lifts himself towards an upright position. 'I'm glad I didn't attempt to go down on a knee or anything.'

Joan is still reflecting. 'How long have I been here?'

Jim sets sights on the door. 'Is it still September?'

'And I arrived in June.'

'About three months then.'

'Three months…' Joan eases himself up from his chair. 'We barely know each other.'

'Three months is a long time in here.' The preciousness of time, of what one does with it, seems increasingly acute as Jim inches towards the exit.

By the time he reaches it, Joan is there to hold it open: this set-to, it seems, will not upset their morning routine. Breakfast in the dining room, sitting in the sitting room and—if it's not raining—a walk in the garden. As they walk up the corridor, each leaning a little more on the other than they might like to entertain, Jim proposes a deviation from the norm. 'Of course, we could even have an open marriage—I know you don't do *heteronormative*.'

It is not a word Jim had even heard, three months earlier. Certainly, it has never passed his lips before. He grew up with the unspoken assumption that he would be more-or-less the same as his parents. And though Dickie had been a man, still they had followed the model set out for them. Theirs had been a marriage in all but name. With its normal roles and normal betrayals: Jim thinks being *open* might not be a bad thing.

Joan thinks it hilarious. 'Girl's not got a lot of choice in this place.'

'Harold?'

'He and Jesus are strictly monogamous.'

And as the lift is rising towards them, Jim joins Joan laughing. For this is why he loves him: a lifetime's adversity has taught Joan to take *nothing* seriously. And when death does come, Joan will share a joke with him.

But for the present time, Jim has his own punchline. 'And just think of the double bed.'

'Now there *is* an incentive.'

And with perfect timing, the doors ping open.

127

Joan

Ah, Ms Ferrier. Voice like brandy. And the strings so outrageously perky as she wonders what she can possibly do without her Eurydice. The Gluck fits my mood this evening—full of contradiction—brain unpicking everything, but hands purl-knit, purl-knit to the beat. How quick it all comes back. My father was quite horrified when I came back from his mother's one weekend, trailing yarn. *What you teach him that for?* he hollered down the phone at her. *Boys don't knit!* Well, this one did. This boy did all the things he shouldn't have—still does.

Purl. *I do not see the point in doing 'the right thing'—especially when the thing in question is in contradiction with one's own instincts.*

Knit. *I do like him.*

Purl. *I do not need a certificate to prove my affection.*

Knit. *I do believe I may love him, even.*

Purl. *I do not have any truck with love—at least, not the sort with extra o's around its midriff.*

Knit. *I do enjoy sleeping with him, although not in a single.*

Purl. *I do not sleep well in a single.*

Purl. *I do not want to get married for a mattress.*

Purl. *I do not approve of jumping through hoops—of the care system, or any other—and besides, the double mattress is mere conjecture.*

A knock at the door interrupts my interior aria.

'Oh yes?' Of course, I know who it is.

'Room service.' And who it isn't.

I attempt to adopt a more upright position—always something of a mission. These days I have pain almost everywhere, almost all the time. But these last few days I've had a particularly persistent one in my sternum. Craigie-Darling helps me raise myself up on cushions. I lower lashes at him. 'Thought I'd have you to myself this evening.'

The blond has grown out and, at sides and back, his curls are more severely buzzed; the scowl doesn't budge. 'You two had a row or something?'

'Joan just needed some Joan time.' I hold my handiwork up for inspection. 'I've decided to take up knitting and give up smoking.' Little does he know I'm having a discreet drag on the balcony every evening. 'What do you think?'

'What is it?'

It is a yellow oblong, quite obviously—knitted with my inheritance from Mary, Mary, Quite Contrary. About time I did something with it. 'Lemon twin set. Age appropriate.'

The face does not crack.

'Nice pearl necklace to go with it.'

Seemingly Jim's not the only one having an off day—that one's been curdling since I left his milk out this morning. This one's halfway blue already. He thrusts the cup towards me. 'Nightcap.'

'Courvoisier?'

'You'll be lucky.'

I take the pills from him before he has opportunity to toss them. No blue one, of course: little does he know it's *Joan of Arc* here who can't make a fire with her wood. 'So, what's up with you tonight?'

He shrugs. 'Got caught.'

'Ah.'

'Yeah.'

'In flagrante delicto?'

Well, that shoots straight over, *my dear*—Craigie's still frowning from ear to ear. 'He looked at my phone.'

Ah, the *mobile*—where secrets pile up, like plastic pill cups in the Pacific; I pass my cup back. 'So…?'

'Dunno. Have to see when I get home.'

Miss Thing has never been exactly forthcoming about *him indoors*: I'm not sure I've been told his name, even. Though my mind is an ocean: treasures lay forgotten at the bottom. But there's nothing wrong with my intuition, and I've been sensing an undertow for some time now. 'What did I tell you—too young to settle.'

'Who says I'm settling for anything?'

Well, that's told me then. The mood this one's in, I can't say I envy his poor husband this evening. 'Do *try* to keep your temper with him.'

And what he's making that face at me for, I've no idea— *he's* the deputy manager who can't manage his own anger. 'Thanks, Gramma.' And then—without so much as a *bye*— he's leaving.

I put a halt to his trajectory. 'Did Jim tell you he proposed to me?'

I'd not planned to tell him. I'd not planned to tell anyone. Who is there to tell, anyway? Gladys, maybe. But I don't need to hear that one going all rose-tinted down the phone line and scolding me for doing the *wrong thing*. The telling somehow makes the marriage a *real thing*—something that could have happened. Could still happen.

'Congratulations!' It's like some hidden stagehand has flown the corners of his mouth towards the ceiling.

'I didn't accept, obviously.'

Lost to the *mammon* of matching morning suits, he has trouble computing this. 'Did you even consider it?'

'Darling, marriage is an antiquated patriarchal institution

designed to control women: why on earth would I give it my consideration?'

On the frontline of Gay Liberation, marriage was *not* one of our demands: back then, even women didn't want it. We did stage a *mock* wedding as protest: there was a fight over who should wear the dress.

'Or perhaps, Joan, marriage—at this time, in this place—is the most radical action you could possibly take?'

I doubletake at this doublethinking.

'I mean, just imagine... Harold, Eileen.'

It's true that—as we get older, as our world shrinks ever smaller—we must work with whatever, or whoever, is in the room.

'You and Jim—you could drag all of them into the twenty-first century, kicking and screaming.'

One tiny action may be the butterfly wing precipitating a hurricane of revolution.

'Wouldn't that be something worth doing?'

The love for one man may be manifestation of a love for *all* men.

'I'm going to ask the husband to be open.' Craig has the door wide, as if to illustrate his proposition.

'And how do you think that'll go down?'

'I hope he will at least—' his voice mimics mine, '—*give it his consideration.*'

He *throws shade* in that way all the young queens are doing. His words are a stuck record long after he's gone, and I am left alone with the needles' clicking.

Knit. *I do think he's right; it's all about context: an old hat out there would seem the most outré millinery in here. One man's present is another man's future: see LGBT rights in Russia.*

Purl. *I do not like the thought of giving my hand to anyone: right or left am I to choose which one? And how will I wield sword or pen or, indeed, needle then?*

Knit. *I do, on the other hand, imagine adherence could come as something of a relief, like stepping into a warm bath—of ass' milk perhaps—after a life spent stepping over asps.*

Purl. *I do not believe exclusion to be compatible with union: the exclusion of others is a colonialist-capitalist construction; othering is something I've spent my whole life fighting.*

My therapist—or one of them, at least—used to suggest I focus on what I can make happen. On the fights I *can* win. Was it Peter or Paul or Michael or Martin with whom I stood squabbling over yards of white satin? It could have been any one of them. I suppose I would have taken any one of them. Had it been a thing then. Had I been less stubborn. Had there not been a plague on. Had there been no competition. This time I'm the only one in the running for the gown.

Knit. *I do love a meringue, especially lemon.*

Another therapist—I forget which—noted that I expect others to reject me when they find I'm not as fabulous as I appear to manifest and all my *many* rejections have been manifestation of this. Like the Dom Pérignon in a shopfront that never wants to be bought or opened because—if it were and turned out really to be Cava—it couldn't bear the disappointment. Mainly with itself.

Knit. *I do enjoy a fizzy wine, whether or not it is champagne.*

My last therapist, I'm thinking—I am now on my last of everything—asserted that my secret terror is *not* that I am not as fabulous as I appear to manifest, but that I *am*. And who am I, really, to be so very extraordinary and so very happy? Like the prize ballroom dancer who will not take the floor because they fear they are unworthy of the joy they will bring. To themselves.

And to those around them.

Knit. *I do want to see Harold try the YMCA—then I may die happy.*

Jim

'And you have informed your niece?'

Ms Mirza is sat behind her desk and Jim is sat before it. 'No, I…' Her picture frames are forming some buttressing between them. 'I'm afraid I've no idea…'

'We don't have her number.' Joan is perching side-saddle next to Jim—as if not yet committing to taking their horse by the mane. 'We were hoping you might do the honours.'

'I shall add that to my list.' She scratches at a pad with a pen.

'Thank you.' Jim smiles, in an attempt at amelioration. 'And what happens then?'

'Then, providing there are no objections…'

'Objections?' Joan's hackles can be heard rising.

'From the family, for instance. An appointment must be made at the register office.'

'I see.' Joan looks at Jim from the corner of an eye.

'And, once you have given notice, you may proceed to book the ceremony.' She dodges the word *marriage*, deftly. 'When are you…?'

'As soon as possible.' Jim looks to Joan for confirmation.

'Yes. Before one of us drops down dead.'

It is taking some recalibration, but Jim is learning that when Joan makes light of things it is often because he is experiencing feelings of the weightiest kind.

Ms Mirza coughs, places down her pen. 'Then I had best also begin the process of transferring the two of you to a double room.' The tone of her voice would seem to suggest that this also is an administrative burden she could well do without.

'I should warn you that there is often a significant waiting list and…'

'And I bet heterosexual couples rise *straight* to the top of it.' Joan shifts even closer to the edge of his seat, poised for fight or flight at any moment.

'No.' Ms Mirza rearranges papers on her desk in a manner which might perhaps indicate that she is not comfortable with any of this, but that she is trying her level best. 'We are in the twenty-first century, Joan. How about you?'

She looks up at him, challenging; Joan says nothing. Jim is also learning that when Joan stays silent it is often because something has struck home. And indeed, Ms Mirza's observation *is* an astute one: Joan does tend to fight the same battles over and again; Jim has noted this in their domestic routines. Right now, he could do without a confrontation—this room is barely big enough for the three of them, without the introduction of oversized emotions—and he finds himself taking unusual interest in an image of domestic bliss in one of the frames on Ms Mirza's desk. It is angled towards him to reveal a woman— white-gowned and smiling—and a man—suited and handsome. Perhaps a young *Mrs* Mirza and her husband.

'I will liaise with Melissa for the time being…'

Jim looks up again as she addresses herself to him.

'Though upon marriage, attorney will pass automatically to Joan.'

'Oh!' Joan jiggles his shoulders to and fro.

Mrs Mirza doesn't look impressed at all. 'As you know, we are small and cater solely to individuals. You will remain with us only until a suitable room becomes available at another institution.'

This comes as a shock. 'But…' It had never occurred to Jim

that the change in their situation might necessitate a change of *location*. 'We don't want to go anywhere else now.'

It's true: they have reached some form of equilibrium with the other residents. And Jim, for one, has no desire to go through the habituation again. Of course, some must have to *come out* day in day out. He has been fortunate—a job for life, just a few changes of neighbour over the years. But at each new introduction, there has always been that nagging question— *when do I tell them? And will they like me less when I do?* There has always been that sense of shame, of feeling *sorry* for *who I am*.

'I am sorry, Jim.' Mrs Mirza is shrugging.

Jim refuses to approach what remains of his life in apologetic fashion; this much Joan has taught him. Reaching for his fiancé's hand like a gear stick, Jim shifts up. '*This* is our home.'

Joan gives Jim's hand a squeeze of approval. Mrs Mirza isn't sure where to look, again inspects her paperwork. And it is then that Jim sees it, the rainbow. At first he thinks it a flare in his lenses but—upon adjusting his glasses—it remains emblazoned on her uppermost document.

The flag is not something Jim has ever had much to do with: he and Dickie never even attended a Pride demonstration. In the early days it had seemed too political; latterly there had seemed too many people. Joan had been scathing on how Pride had moved from protest to marketplace but still, Jim wishes he might have played some small part. He will not dwell on it: he will live—*what is it that Craig always says*—his *best life* in the present.

'It is reassuring you now feel at home.' Mrs Mirza speaks slowly, as if choosing words individually. 'But I cannot just conjure up a double room.'

In the past, Jim might have just accepted *that was that*. But now he is learning not to *take things lying down*, and when to see the funny side of them. 'What about a double *bed*? Could your conjuring skills stretch to that?'

She laughs hollowly. 'That will not be possible. I am sorry.' And again, she turns away—this time to her monitor—quartered into sitting room, dining room, corridor, garden. Perhaps she spots something troubling in those surveillance monochromes—perhaps Maude has taken in an injured fledgling, as she had back in summertime, and Anya is wailing to have found her foot spa repurposed as bird bath again—because now Mrs Mirza is frowning.

'That's that then.' Joan removes his hand from Jim's, makes to stand. This is his way: leave the room and throw colourful, combustible cocktails from outside in until the enemy capitulates completely.

Jim prefers to stay, negotiate compromises. Looking down at his empty hand, an idea strikes him—almost with the clarity of a clock chiming—and—without allowing himself a hesitation, now that he is living in the moment—he stretches and slips the gold-links from about his wrist. 'I believe this should cover it.'

He places the watch on her desk. It makes a satisfying clunk on impact: it had not been cheap, far from it, when he bought it. And it is now, like him, an antique—in the absence of access to his own life savings, he must barter with such riches as he can rally from about his person and surely it must be worth enough, more than enough, to purchase a decent double mattress.

'That was Dickie's.' Joan is now frowning.

But Jim maintains momentum; his future is with the man sat beside him, not with… 'Dickie doesn't need it.'

Mrs Mirza is shaking her head. 'I cannot…'

Jim isn't having it. 'But *we* need a bed. Queen size,

orthopaedic.' He feels like he is at that market again—he cannot remember where or when or even what he was buying—Dickie was beside him and they had both hated the idea of haggling but then, once Jim began... He had felt the blood coursing along veins; he feels it again: the exhilaration of abandoning the rules and regulations his life has revolved around, like riding without reins.

'I am sorry, Jim.' Mrs Mirza pushes the watch back towards him. 'There are strict guidelines on such things.'

And he is thrown then.

She sits a moment, reading his disappointment; it seems she is reaching for a decision. 'It is unorthodox but...' She reaches again for her pen. 'There are perhaps funds we might access. I shall add it to my list to discuss with your niece.' She writes another note, punctuates it with a full-stop.

Joan retrieves the watch. 'Darling, don't worry—when I have power of attorney, you shall have ALL the orthopaedic mattresses.' He delicately slips the watch back upon Jim's wrist.

'I am sure that, between us, we shall see your bed is sorted and...' Mrs Mirza caps her pen. 'I am sure I speak for everyone in saying we shall be glad to have you staying.'

Jim has always loved this moment—when one knows one has got the contract, even if one doesn't know quite how one has got it. 'Thank you.'

'Thanks.' Joan retakes Jim's hand. 'Of course, we'll keep both rooms.'

'Use mine as the master bedroom and yours as a...'

'Dressing room. Secret passage between the two.'

Even Mrs Mirza is laughing now. 'I do not think a passage will be possible.'

'Then perhaps a little glory hole?' Joan bites his lip like

Barbara Windsor after having let fly her bra.

'I shall leave that to your discretion.' If she knows what he means, she does not let on. 'Was there anything else, gentlemen?'

Jim has everything he ever wanted.

'Yes.' Joan smiles in that mischievous way of his, slips a bangle from his wrist. 'Perhaps you might accept this as a *personal* gift—offset your eyes, I think.' Its stones are not precious, but they are precious to him. 'And another, for dear Melissa.' He slips off a second. 'Kindly forward it to her as a token of my esteem.' He places his diamantes down, along with his demands. 'We'd like a reception, here in the home. Fizzy wine, disco dancing, and all the trimmings.'

Jim is smiling—*every winner needs a wingman.*

'We'd like to arrive in a chauffeur-driven limousine decked out in pink ribbons. A rainbow-coloured *congratulations* hanging in the sitting room.'

Jim's smile broadens—*never too late, then.*

'We'd like to invite all the staff and residents and—oh, please say you'll do it—we'd like you to give a speech!'

Mrs Mirza's eyebrows appear to have got hooked up in the hem of her headscarf.

And Jim's smile hooks from one ear to the other.

Joan

Well, it's not a limousine but it is pink-ribboned, chauffeur-driven. This time—at my insistence—Mister Minibus driver *does* play Wagner. Not that oft-used thing from Lohengrin: the Valkyries are riding as we ride home, all guns blazing. Like that film. *What was it called again?* Set in Vietnam. Anyway, Mister Driver daren't look anywhere but the road in front of him, and is sweating disapproval from every pore of his being. And I'm sure, then, that we're doing the right thing.

I did have a little wobble, back in the registry office. We'd had the music—for me, *Song to the Moon*, *Fly Me to the Moon* for Jim—and the readings—classic Shakespeare sonnet, him, and me, a free-form Walt Whitman—and then, when Jim had said his piece—with, it should be said, barely a crease—my big finish—*I, John*—this being all legit, we were using the names on our birth certificates—*I, John Robert Crawford, take you, James Edward Brown to be my lawful wedded husband.* Well, the words just wouldn't come. And inside my head there's this whole production going on—my life staged before me in a second—and it can only have been a second, because Jim is still stood there, smiling—and I'm thinking *what the fuck are you doing, my dear, what the fuck are you doing here—all those freedoms we fought for sacrificed on this lectern-cum-altar?* And I'm still looking at Jim, and Jim is still smiling, and then the words to the poem come back to me again—*I carry my old delicious burdens, I carry them with me wherever I go*—and I do, I so do—*I give you myself before preaching or law; will you give me yourself? will you come travel with me?*

A burden—whether delicious or otherwise—will be lessened when shared, and two may travel further than one alone. I have always wanted to go as far as possible. So I say *I do*—right there in that riotously-carpeted registry office with Craig and Gladys for witness.

The pair of them are now in the backseat, screeching away as gravel screeches beneath us on the driveway. The trees on either side were lime-green when I first pulled in here; now they're all but bare.

Craig slides the door open. Looks a dream—dickie bow and braces matching. Gladys has taken quite the shine: she's right up and after him. She's wearing a shiny trouser-suit and saucy bonnet—pill box with the net down front, court shoes to match. Nearly goes over on them as she leaps onto uneven ground. Or possibly this is a ploy to feel the firmness of Craig's hand.

Jim is next out, looking dashing—suit, waistcoat, everything. Cravat and buttonhole (of course) matching. He is lemon to my meringue topping. Gladys found it in a charity shop for next-to-nothing, veil included. Few tucks and nips and fits me perfect. Though it only comes to just above *my* nips, so the November temperature comes as something of a shock. And my sliver of silver chest hair does little to fend it off. As I step from within, Gladys extends her hand like some jumped-up lady-in-waiting. I take it, with appreciation: if I go over now, I may never get up again. This frock is trip-hazard incarnate so, unlike Gladys, I'm wearing a sensible flat. I did ask Jim if he'd prefer a sensible *suit*. He said he'd spent his whole life being sensible and look where it had got him. *The old-people's home.* So here I am, looking like a pantomime dame in the resolution scene, carnations the colour of ripe cheddar in my hand.

'Say cheese!'

Craig's got the phone out. Snap, snap, snap. Got us lined up on the porch—bouquet and buttonhole match brickwork a treat. The pics will be over the internet before we know it. They'll either *love it* or they'll *hate it*, all those twittergrammers. Either way, it's good PR: couple of old dears camping it up at the care home door.

After we enter, it's a bit of a blur. Not sure if that's adrenalin or painkillers.

'Congratulations, Uncle Jim!'

In reception, two women.

'Thank you, um…' He's struggling.

I step in. 'Melissa!' As in *McCarthy*. As in *Bridesmaids*. (No longer am I *ever the*).

Jim's niece reels him in for an embrace, which he awkwardly reciprocates. 'So sorry we didn't make the ceremony. Nightmare journey. Just off the train. Congratulations, Joan!'

Keen not to be enveloped similarly, on taking her hand I immediately curtsy. 'Please, call me Auntie.'

She barks with laughter, whispers. 'Enjoy that bed later.' She then indicates the woman beside her—younger, taller, less severe than her mother. 'This is Jacqueline.'

Aha, my trans great-niece-in-law!

'So it is.' Jim takes her hand and raises it to his lips.

'Is he always such a gentleman?' Jacqueline winks in my direction. 'That dress looks amazing.'

In the sitting room, we're greeted by the self-appointed residents' welcoming committee; the others are objecting, conscientiously. Maude is lobbing confetti as directly as I imagine she might lobby some quaintly reactionary MP; Anya's confetti seems to land mostly on her, rather than me. There's a banner screaming colour above them: someone's been down Poundland.

'Congratulations.'

Madam Mirza seconds its message. She's wearing a kind of kaftan—lovely embroidery, and headscarf matching. She offers us each a firm shake of the hand. 'What lovely rings!' We are wearing matching rhinestone, citrine. He'd wanted to do it 'properly' with jewels and carats. On that, Melissa and I were in agreement; we got these on eBay, two for ten pound. They probably won't last long. But then probably neither will we. I do not mean maritally.

'Let's get this party started, then!'

Craig lets fly a cork across the room. Madam screams and holds her hands up as he ejaculates the fizzy stuff all over us. It is rather thoughtless, when you think about it—what with her being a Muslim. And into this chaos comes Eileen.

'It's all wrong!

Again, confirmation that we're doing the right thing.

'Marriage is a man and a woman!'

She's standing, hands on hips, in the doorway. I can see this could turn nasty, and I'm not about to have my big scene upstaged by some old teabag-lady; I need to act quickly. I toss my bouquet over shoulder…

'You can't just shove it in our faces and…'

It hits her smack in the jaw. She rugby tackles it to the floor. Everyone applauds. I join in. 'That means you're next, Eileen!' She bursts into tears, a harridan tamed. Madam thrusts a beaker of bubbly into her hand, and it's straight down Eileen's gullet before Craig has even had the *chance* to raise a toast up.

'To Joan and Jim!'

And then it's through to the dining room for 'breakfast'—all sausages-on-sticks and, centre-spread, one of those three-tiered things with two grooms, lopsided. Even Harold can't resist once finger-food is served: he zimmers in, eyeing proceedings with suspicion until Princess Eugenia swoops over, proffering a plate piled with fried things. He can't help smiling; I can't help prying. 'What are those, then?'

'Small chop.' His big mouth is full of them. 'Puff puff and plantain.'

'I shall have to try them.'

'Proper Nigerian. Just like Mummy make them.'

The Princess is resting now-empty hands on a bump, evident beneath her tabard. 'We cater for *all* taste here—is that not so, Joan?'

I take one of everything, but with this corset on, I'm having a hard time trying to fit *anything* in. Everyone else is back for seconds, thirded by cake-cutting and speech-making. Gladys does her best-person best to make me blush with recollection of the time I founded a drag commune, then—days later—disbanded it, remarking how *wonderful* it is that someone has finally shown me how to share my sequins. Laughs all round. Craig waxes lyrical about intergenerational learning: he may have shown us old'uns how to get online but we have shown him how to *get off* again. From the chorus of cooing, I suspect I am the only one who gets his double meaning. And finally, the tear-jerker from Madam Mirza: how she lost all her family to civil war, fled Syria, sought asylum here and—having no youngsters of her own—threw herself into caring for our *older* generation, to give them the sort-of send off denied to her parents.

'To care, by definition, is to treat another's concerns as if they were one's own.' Her notes shake in her hand. 'As if carer and cared-for are *one and the same*.' She abandons them. 'I have come to realise I had not been treating everyone the same…'

And I am coming to realise I cut my bias wrong about this woman.

'The prejudices shown to me... as a woman... as a Muslim...'

When I should know better than anyone about prejudice and its patterns.

'They are no different to those shown to men such as Jim... such as Joan.'

Well. I did not weep on exchanging vows, or rings. But now I am bawling like it's my first Oscar win. And I'm not the only one whose spot has been hit: as Jim slips me his lemon handkerchief, I can hear his niece and great-niece snuffling in stereo in the back row.

And then it's back to the sitting room. The chairs have been usurped from their usual positions: Eileen seems uncertain which she may sit on, as a woman. On his trolley service, DJ Craigie has decks rigged up; he's coughing down the microphone.

'And now we'd like to invite the groom and groom to lead off the dancing.'

I am surprised by the opening *pizzicati* of one of Tchaikovsky's many *valses*. I turn to Jim. 'Have you been raiding my record collection?'

'I may have been.' Jim offers his hand.

I feel the weight of expectation. And of judgement. From those seated at the sides of this room. From those no longer even *in the room*. Peter, Paul. Victor. From those I can no longer remember. From those I never even knew, who never had this choice—through years, through millennia. From those who still don't have this choice, in countries near and far. From those who chose not to be here—the mothers, fathers, sisters, brothers—who choose not to celebrate, to share. They're all out there somewhere. Past and future.

'Will you be the woman?' Jim brings me back to present again.

'Can't I just be Joan?' I suppose that's all I ever really wanted: to be myself, and to be loved for it.

At work, I always loved to watch them waltzing—those tights showed *everything*. But when it came to dancing myself, I was more a rock 'n' roller, a swinger, a disco-diva, a raver. Jim on the other hand, loves a bit of ballroom: I can just imagine him and Dickie swishing round the living room, curtains drawn. So of course, I end up following.

'Does this mean I'm finally a swan?'

'You were never an ugly duckling.'

And there you have it—I am loved as I am. As we keep dancing, the others keep joining. First, Madam and Miss Thing—she is as marionette-rigid as Craig is limp-wristed. Next up—in heels and backwards—Gladys partnered with—whoever would've guessed it—Our Lady of the Teabag. Gladys' face is all *it should've been me,* but Eileen looks like the cat that finally got some cream, and is cinching Gladys' waist more closely than may, strictly speaking, be necessary. Harold looks like a schoolboy who got to slow dance the teacher he's been crushing on all year: the princess has him up and pressed against her bump. It is not the YMCA but I'll settle for it. Another, older, mother takes the floor with her unexpected daughter, and last, with muscular thrusts, Maude is circling in her wheelchair; Anya is circling around her. The arms are out; the head is up. The hands, wing-like, swoop the air; the feet glide as though webbed and through water. As if she were once a ballerina.

We were all something before. We are all something more than what we currently are. And maybe it's the aspirin and cheap wine and corseting but for a moment it feels like we're all part of the same choreographed corps, and those cheap flashing things Craig now has going are our stage lighting, this living room our world to play upon. Man, woman. Joan.

'Mmm…'

Back in the dressing room, we crash on our new double mattress. It is so big that everything else—nightstands excepted—has been ejected. So big that they had trouble *getting it in.* Imagine—the delivery men sweating and swearing over a bed for two blokes the same age as their grandads. *How delicious is that?*

I take Jim's hand; we are paper-chained. 'Queen size.'

'Orthopaedic.'

I grip Jim's hand.

'What's wrong?'

Backgrounded all afternoon, the sensation in my sternum has forced itself to the fore again. And I feel a dizzying disassociation—as if I must zoom out from my body to get some distance from the pain. I wave off Jim's concerns. 'Too much rich food and dancing.'

'You didn't eat anything.'

Before he can delve any deeper, there's a knock at the door.

'Oh yes?'

It opens ajar; a voice emerges from behind it. 'Is this the bridal suite?'

'I'm afraid we've not broken the hymen yet.'

My *husband* can be quite funny when he puts his mind to it.

Craig negotiates the perimeter of our marital bedstead. 'I have something that might help with that.' Jim's nightcap has a shot of blue in it. 'You've *both* got one extra tonight.' As does mine—and from the way Miss Thing's misdirecting, I would

147

say he's hiding another addition. 'Oh and…' He places it on my nightstand. 'I made you a present.'

The grooms now stand atop a smaller, browner cake.

'Is that…?' *Hash*, I lipsync.

He winks back. 'Only the finest ingredients.'

'De-lish.'

'Don't tell Madam.'

'Thank you.' Jim has no idea, I'm sure, what he's thanking Craig for. 'Thanks for everything.' He extends his hand. 'Best wishes from me and my husband to you and your husband.'

'I shall extend them.' Craig winks at me again. 'We've *also* got an extra one this evening.'

We scrolled options on his phone a few nights back. 'The ginger?' A red-head had been my favourite.

'Nah, we went for the brunette.'

'Well, don't do anything I wouldn't.'

'Don't leave much, does it?' He sticks his tongue in a cheek.

'Then be sure to be safe about it.'

He waves me off. 'I'm on the PrEP now, innit?' And he waves us both goodnight.

As the door shuts behind him, Jim returns to his concerns. 'How are you feeling?'

'I'm fine.' It's true, the pain has receded to the back of my body again. And I'm getting something of a second wind at the thought of those embellishments on the nightstand.

'I don't suppose this thing is helping.' He indicates the corset. 'Why don't I…' He glimmers an eye. 'Help you out of it?'

'Such a sweet man.' I roll over for him. 'Where have you been all my lifetime?' The truth is less saccharine: he might have been any of the many men who came, key in hand.

'I'm here now, Joan.' He is all thumbs as he attempts to

unfasten my bonds. 'How do you undo this thing?'

My portcullis has been gilded, glittering as the portal to some subterranean kingdom. But never before have I allowed it to be, simply, open.

Jim

Beneath him, the seabed is a riot of pattern: sunlight printing waveforms onto coral-coloured sands with starfish detailing. It's like the floor of Joan's room. And there, of course, is Joan—ultramarine fishtail fanning, shell-combing his last strands. More surprisingly, Dickie is there too—planting cockle shells and silver seaweeds in rows. Jim waves at them, but they do not see him. He tries to swim closer, but the current is against him. Suddenly the sea turns obsidian—a cloud has passed over the sun, or a predator is above him. And Jim remembers he is diving, that his lungs are bursting, that he must struggle to the surface for oxygen.

His head bobs into consciousness from night's dark ocean; he has twice as much to lose in the split second between sleeping and waking: neither of them has surfaced with him.

He lays alone and adrift on the double mattress. That painting floats into his head—they saw it somewhere—maybe the Louvre, something to do with Medusa. A sky of ochre and umber, waves of sage and pewter, and on the raft an old man cradling the body of his dead companion. Only, in Jim's imagination, it is Joan lying wooden in his arms.

Jim had thought him just cold at first, on that winter morning, only a few weeks back. Then, fearing the worst but refusing to believe it, he'd tried to remember all they'd instructed on that first-aid course he'd taken at the office and he tried to kiss life into Joan's blue lips, bellow breath into Joan's ivory chest, but he just wasn't good enough, he just couldn't do it. So he had rung the alarm and sat sobbing as women buzzed in and around them, but he would not he would not let go of Joan's hand, until they prized it from his own and Mrs Mirza cradled Jim to her breast as the princess raised the duvet over Joan's head.

It was Joan's heart, the doctor had told Jim, that won the 'competition'. And somehow this seems fitting. Joan had given his life both barrels; it is no surprise that organ had given out before Jim's.

He thinks about mooring; mornings are arriving each day earlier, for spring is almost here, and he is sure he need not pull into harbour for at least a moment more. Some days he wonders if he need anchor at all. But today there is something he must do.

With heroic effort, he rows himself to shore—pulling back covers, placing feet on *dry floor*. Reaching for his glasses on the nightstand, he finds the two of them looking out at him from within their own frames: Dickie in the dusk of life, Joan in the midday of his—placard, hot, overhead.

All Jim has ever wanted from his own life, really, is to have someone to look out for him. To have someone to look out for.

'And now, you must look out for each other.'

He has been lucky: he has loved, twice over. And although he does not believe in anything more than what we have here, still it comforts him to imagine that something of the two of them might be out there somehow, somewhere. As he drags on his dressing gown, he is even smiling at the thought of their meeting. *Now that's a conversation he wouldn't mind overhearing.*

The sounds of a different exchange rise from the garden. He cannot see them but, again, finds it comforting to know they, at least, are still with him. *Little vixens.* Joan's beloved roses are now nothing but thorns, but the ground around them is flecked saffron, as crocuses come into bloom. Joan would have loved

151

those, too. If only he had seen them. If only they had had more time. And not for the first time, Jim stands there wishing—as he rubs his ring, with its *costume citrine*—before taking himself in hand, and taking himself next door, to begin the always arduous process of dressing.

Soon they will want it back, he is certain, but for now the *dressing room* is still Joan's room. And Joan's things are still everywhere. Jim hasn't yet had it in him to do anything with them. *What is he to do with them?* Certainly, he can't keep *all* of them. Not in one little room. *Perhaps Jacqueline might like some clothing? Perhaps Craig could put the records online?* Jim supposes they would be worth something.

One LP is still mounted on its player: it is the one Joan played more than all the others. The one he played once for Jim, roughly translating the German as Jessye Norman sang *Four Last Songs*. Jim had found it rather too rich for him. But—for Joan—he spins it again.

He listens to the first song, the second and the third song as he puts his suit on; he has only the one of them, the same suit he wore for the wedding. The same shirt, the same shoes, though the tie is different. A simple black one. But the simple task of tying it eludes him. He moves to the mirror—concentrates on this everyday act, once so automatic, finds he can no longer do it.

And really, *what is the point? Who is this person in the mirror and why are they still here, when there is no one to look out for them and no one for them to look out for?* And there is just the hiss and crackle of old vinyl in his ears. Then the music again soars.

It is the fourth of those *Four Last Songs*. Joan's absolute favourite. Something about sunset. And the music transforms the morning. Just as the sun, on setting, transforms the sky from humdrum cerulean into symphonies of cadmium—yellow, red, orange—

briefly and brilliantly burning before a lamp black oblivion.

Joan had been his sun. Jim can never be just cerulean again.

He returns to the wardrobe for the cravat he wore as groom. Pre-tied. Lemon. He clips it on. He pulls the tangerine chiffon from the light-fitting. Repurposes it as pocket handkerchief. And on the dressing table, Joan's crimson lipstick. Jim reaches for it, removes the lid. Winds it up as he'd watched Joan doing, has no idea what to do with it then.

He stands, looking in the mirror. Sees *that person*. Perhaps Jim might try looking out for him.

There is a knock at the door. 'Come in.' Jim does not turn from his reflection but sees behind him that Craig is wearing a black jacket over his usual blue uniform.

'The bus is loaded. Even Harold.' He smiles tightly. 'Your niece and her daughter are going to meet us there. So we're ready when you are.'

Jim turns to him then. 'Do you know how to put this on?'

Craig looks at the lipstick in Jim's hand, looks at Jim. He nods almost imperceptibly, takes the lipstick from Jim, towers over him, lips stretching—as though he has a finger hooked in each corner of his grin. Jim understands he is to do the same and senses Craig's hands shaking as he applies the stick to top then bottom lip. Probably it will be all wonky. But then, really, isn't that just exactly as it should be? All his life Jim has scrubbed up admirably but inside, hasn't he always been *a bit wonky*?

'There.'

Craig rubs his lips together. Again, Jim understands he must do the same. His lips feel claggy, taste like the wax crayons he lay chewing on the nursery floor as he tried to decide what next to draw. *What next can he possibly draw?*

He draws himself upright, turns back to the mirror.

How bizarre. A monochrome man emblazoned with Joan's cadmiums—the embers of a fire, still stubbornly burning.

Joan would always find *something* to draw upon.

Jim is startled from his reflections by the sound of a lipstick being recapped, replaced on the cabinet. He looks up to see Craig's lips—emboldened by cadmium—smiling, more broadly this time. And Jim smiles back at him. None of them will ever be just cerulean again.

Craig offers his arm. Jim takes it. And as they exit, the music plays out: the orchestra descending and descending and, above them, two flutes trilling; as night is falling, in the day's evanescence, two birds.

Singing.

Acknowledgements

To my publisher, Justin David, who has believed in this story in all its incarnations, and encouraged me to give it one last shot in fictional form.

To my editor Alex Hopkins, who was the first person I entrusted with this manuscript, and the only person I would have wanted to help me put the finishing touches to it.

To Leather Lane Writers, whose feedback has helped shape every chapter—Katy Whitehead, Hugo Bennett, Neil Lawrence, Joshua Davis, Niki Seth-Smith, Lisa Goldman, and Bart Bennett—who also did a fine (toothed) job of proofing the book.

To Daren Kay, for his ever-witty copy; to Derek Benton, for his fabulous fluting on the trailer soundtrack; to Andy Pisanu, for sharing his studio so we could record our first audiobook.

To the actors who breathed life into earlier incarnations of these characters, in readings and stagings—Lavinia Co-op, John Atterbury, David Meyer, Nathaniel Campbell, Alexis Gregory, Bette Bourne, Richard Wilson, Chris New, Nina Wadia, Joseph Mydell and Georgina Hale.

To casting director Gary Davy and producer Raiomond Mirza who did everything in their power to bring *The Grey Liberation Front* to the silver screen; to producer Clarisse M. Kye and publicist Anna Goodman for bringing *SwanSong* before a real live audience.

To Octavia Housing Trust, Opening Doors London, Stuart Feather, Sarah Durbridge and Sherree Peake for their help with research.

To friends and family who've offered writing sanctuary—especially Liz Norton in St Leonards, Anthony Psaila in Margate, Tim Redfern in Rye, Mum and Dad in Brittany.

To all those who would not accept defeat, and through whom we may all now live in spectrum.

Also from Inkandescent

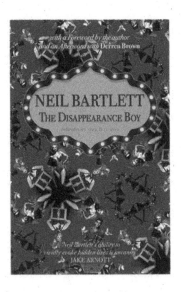

www.inkandescent.co.uk

Also from Inkandescent

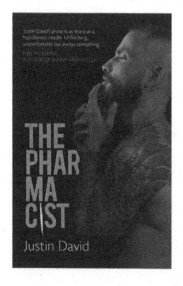
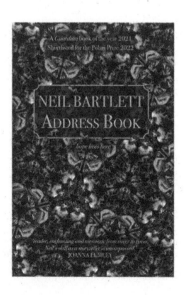

www.inkandescent.co.uk

by outsiders for outsiders

Inkandescent Publishing was created in 2016
by Justin David and Nathan Evans to shine a light on
diverse and distinctive voices.

Could you do one more Inkredible thing for us?
Sign up to our mailing list to stay informed
about future releases:

www.inkandescent.co.uk/sign-up

follow us on Facebook:

@InkandescentPublishing

on Twitter:

@InkandescentUK

on Threads:

@inkandescentuk

and on Instagram:

@inkandescentuk